Joe remembered he'd switched rooms....

Bleary-eyed, he shook his head to clear it, and recalled the right number. Forty-seven-eighty-two.

That was it. The key card clicked and the door opened with ease.

Wow, he was more tired than he realized.

The king-size bed awaited. He shucked his jeans and tossed his shirt to the floor, crawled onto the soft mattress and was asleep as soon as his head hit the pillow.

Still, even in his dreams he couldn't get Carly out of his mind. The piercing blue eyes, the sexy curves.

Her spicy scent filled his senses. He felt her soft breasts pushing against his back. In his dream he turned over and wrapped his arms around her hot body. It seemed so real that he could've sworn he could feel the silky material of her top. He nuzzled into a sweet neck, pressed a kiss to her delicate skin and heard her moan.

He stilled. Forced his heavy lids to open. And looked right into the wide-open eyes of Carly...

Dear Reader,

I've been intrigued with the "wrong bed" concept in romance novels for a long time. And I wanted to see if I could write one that was believable. The key ingredient to making two people end up in the same bed by mistake seemed to me to be two bedrooms that looked exactly alike. I immediately thought of the cruise my family and I took. On the ship, every hallway on every deck looks exactly like the others, and every cabin, too. Perfect. And what more romantic setting could there be than the lush islands of the Caribbean?

The next ingredient for this story was getting a laid-back firefighter to melt the hardened heart of a tough, ambitious New Yorker. And, of course, the key to every great romance is always love. Love to bring together two people who appear to have nothing in common. Love to heal a lonely childhood and a broken heart. Love to give two people the courage to forgive the past and make a fresh start.

I hope this Wrong Bed story works for you! Watch for the next two books in this series coming soon, and please check my website, www.jillianburns.com, for more info and excerpts. Here's a hint: I'm researching Navy SEALs.

Happy reading!

Jillian Burns

Cabin Fever

—

Jillian Burns

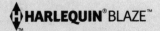

Recycling programs
for this product may
not exist in your area.

ISBN-13: 978-0-373-79817-9

CABIN FEVER

Printed in U.S.A.

ABOUT THE AUTHOR

Jillian Burns fell in love while reading such classics as *Jane Eyre* and *Pride and Prejudice* in her teens and has been reading romance novels ever since. She lives in Texas with her husband of twenty-five years and their three half-grown kids. She likes to think her emotional nature—sometimes referred to as moodiness by those closest to her—has found the perfect outlet in writing stories filled with passion and romance. She believes romance novels have the power to change lives with their message of eternal love and hope.

Books by Jillian Burns

HARLEQUIN BLAZE
466—LET IT RIDE
577—SEDUCE AND RESCUE
602—PRIMAL CALLING
621—BY INVITATION ONLY
    "Secret Encounter"
634—NIGHT MANEUVERS
670—ONCE A HERO
733—RELENTLESS SEDUCTION

To get the inside scoop on Harlequin Blaze and its talented writers, be sure to check out blazeauthors.com.

All backlist available in ebook format.

For my husband and partner of twenty-five years. You may not be "Mr. Romance," but you are always there for me. And that's true love.

A huge debt of gratitude goes to the usual suspects, without whom I could not produce even one chapter: Pam, Linda, Von, Barb and my editor, Kathryn Lye.

1

"YOU'RE LYING, TEDESCO."

Joe narrowed his eyes at his accuser, brought the can of root beer to his lips and took a long sip. "You'll have to play to find out, Wakowski."

Wakowski snarled and studied his dwindling pile of chips on the table in the fire station's kitchen.

Joe tapped his fingers on his thigh. With his luck they'd get a call before he could lay down his cards.

"Come on, Wakowski," Everman urged. "In this century." Everman had already folded, as had Miller and Stockton. Joe maintained his poker face.

Wakowski narrowed his eyes. "You're bluffing." He shoved all his remaining chips into the center of the table.

Joe grinned and revealed his Queen-high heart flush. "Read 'em and weep."

The guys whooped and hollered and thudded Joe on the back. Wakowski cursed and pitched his cards down. "You're a real scootch, you know dat?"

Joe grinned and began gathering up his winnings. His cell buzzed and he grabbed it off the table. At two on a Saturday afternoon it was probably his mother calling to make sure he was coming to the family dinner tomorrow. He checked the caller ID, but he didn't recognize the number. He hesitated answering. If one of his sisters had set him up with one of their friends again…

Knowing he'd regret it, he punched the answer button. "Tedesco."

"Mr. *Joe* Tedesco, of Brooklyn, New York?"

Great. Were telemarketers allowed to call cell phones now? "Uh…yeah?"

"This is *Carly's Couture* calling about your entry in The Sexiest Average Joe contest and I'm thrilled to tell you that you are our winner!"

Joe blinked. Contest? Sexiest what? Wait a minute… He grinned at his fellow firemen sitting around the station house table. "Good one, guys." He spoke into the phone. "So, I won, huh? What'd I win? A hot and heavy night with you, sweetheart?"

"Excuse me?"

Joe winced. The sleet falling outside was no match for the ice in this woman's voice. If this was a prank, she was really good. "Uh, hold on a sec." He held the phone to his chest. "Okay, you guys, you might as well fess up. I'm not falling for it."

All four of his buddies gave him a confused look. Not good. He put the phone back to his ear. "Who'd you say you were again?"

"Carly Pendleton, with *Carly's Couture*. I have a fashion blog for the average man and woman, and *Mo-*

diste magazine cosponsored the national contest searching for the Sexiest Average Joe."

Fashion blog? Wait. *Modiste?* Wasn't that the fancy magazine his sisters were always reading, with all the makeover contests and quizzes on how to please a guy in bed? Alarm bells clanged and they weren't coming from the firehouse. Joe stood and paced from the kitchen into the common area.

"Mr. Tedesco? Are you there?"

He barely heard her voice. Her previous words kept echoing in his mind. Contest. *Modiste* magazine. What had his sisters done now?

He cleared his throat. "Yeah, I'm here." Maybe he should think positive. Maybe he'd won a big-screen TV or a year's supply of beer.

"—and the cruise leaves on Monday. I'll have your boarding pass and a car will pick you up at your residence at 7:00 a.m. The flight to Miami departs at ten. The ship sails at four. Now, your entry form said you already have a passport?"

"Wait a minute. I won a cruise?" That could be fun.

"Five days and four nights to the Caribbean. Of course, that's where we'll be doing the photo shoot."

"Photo shoot?"

The woman mumbled a request to save her from idiots. "You *did* read all the details of the contest before entering, didn't you, Mr. Tedesco?"

He clenched his teeth. "It's Joe. Mr. Tedesco is my father."

"Okay. In case you need reminding, *Joe,* the photo shoot is the reason for the cruise. My blog will feature the Sexiest Average Joe wearing *Carly's Couture* clothing choices and posing with a beautiful supermodel in exotic locales. You could end up with a lucrative modeling career, Mr. Tedesco. Maybe even become famous."

Famous? If he'd wanted money and fame he would've signed the contract offer his sophomore year. He sure as hell wasn't posing for some magazine like one of those pretty boys strutting around in their underwear. No, thanks. "Look, lady, I can't just take off work at a moment's notice."

"Mr. Te—Joe. I promise the shoot won't take all your time. There'll be excursions and nightlife and we even provide you fifty dollars' worth of chips at the ship's casino."

"You could offer me a thousand dollars in chips and I still wouldn't be posing for some women's magazine, especially not for some sexiest-man photos."

"Oh, ho! Sexiest man?" called Everman.

Joe swiveled to find his fellow firemen gathered around him.

"Whoa, Mr. Sexy, huh?" Miller mocked.

Wakowski locked his hands behind his head and wiggled his hips. "Oooh, Sexy Joey."

Joe shut them down with a scowl and an obscene hand gesture.

A split second of silence on the other end of the line suggested that the lady had heard the background commotion. "Look, Mr. Tedesco. When you signed the entry form you agreed to all the terms and conditions of the contest."

Joe balled his free hand into a fist. "I didn't sign anything. I don't even know what you're talking about."

"Really? Then, whoever did sign your name on the entry forms could be prosecuted for forgery."

"Now hold on a minute." His sisters were going to pay for this. The entry had to be their doing. He couldn't see any of the guys here at the station risking his wrath. Or ever reading *Modiste* magazine for that matter. But he couldn't let Donna-Marie and Rosalie be brought up on charges. He sighed. The chief had been nagging him to take some of his vacation....

"I'll talk to my boss about the time off. If I'm able, I'll be ready at 7:00 a.m. Monday."

"Oh, that's wonderful, Mr.—Joe. I promise you're going to have a wonderful week in the Caribbean."

Joe clicked off, ignored his buddies' questions and stalked toward the chief's office. A wonderful week? He seriously doubted that.

CARLY STOOD FUMING in Miami's cruise terminal, slapping her clipboard against her linen skirt-covered thigh. For five long years she'd slaved away as a seamstress in the garment district learning everything she could about the fashion industry. Her interactive blog had only allowed her to quit her day job just last year. It was doing well, but this was her shot to hit the big time.

And the supermodel was late.

Unfortunately, she'd sent the same limo this morning to pick up her Average Joe. She'd had to scramble at the last minute to book them the next flight to Miami and hope they made that one. Then arrange for the Florida limo to return for them once they reached Miami International Airport.

After arriving at the cruise terminal, Carly had successfully directed the photographer and his crew, the hair and makeup teams, the *Modiste* liaison and the clothing handlers from the major department stores on Fifth Avenue onto the ship. All of the top stores had agreed, thanks to the editor at *Modiste,* to lend couture for the shoots. But the clothes would do no good if the ship took off without her models.

She pulled her cell out and called the limo service one more time. They'd already contacted the driver once and confirmed the limo was waiting for the plane to land. Piper—the supermodel with one name, had kept the limo waiting to take her to JFK airport for over three hours. She'd barely made the following flight out.

And if they didn't get to the cruise terminal in the next thirty minutes, the ship would sail without them.

"Ms. Pendleton, the driver reported he's five blocks from the pier."

"Thank you!" She touched End Call on her screen, stuck her phone back in her jacket pocket, and ran as fast as her Louboutins would carry her to the terminal entrance.

Within a few minutes she saw the limo pull up and the driver get out and open the back door. Out stepped the most exotically beautiful woman Carly had ever seen. Straight black hair fell to her waist and her soft caramel complexion showed off luminous light green eyes that looked around her with distaste. The woman carried an enormous handbag and a tiny yappy dog.

Beside her was a shorter woman holding a diamond-studded leash. Piper's assistant. Carly had spoken with her on the phone. She had the same exotic features as Piper. Beautiful, even with the left side of her face marred by a long, jagged scar.

When the assistant turned her left side away, Carly could've kicked herself for staring, and searched behind the two women for her Average Joe.

Where was he?

The driver was at the trunk unloading six, no, seven pieces of designer luggage. And helping him while they talked as if they'd been good friends for years was her contest winner.

Her breath caught as Joe smiled at something the driver said. Carly usually detested the scruffy, unshaved look that was popular right now, wishing she could take a razor to their jaw. But on her Average Joe, it worked, befitting his blue-collar status and accenting his white teeth.

"Hello?" The supermodel snapped her fingers in front of Carly's face.

Annoyed at herself, Carly stepped forward and extended her right hand. "Piper, so nice to meet you." The dog snapped at her fingers and Carly jerked her hand back just in time to prevent getting bit. The dog's high-pitched yapping made her ears ring.

"Oh, poor Pootsie! You've upset him." Piper's low, smoky voice still managed to sound whiny, even with the British accent.

Carly bit the inside of her cheek and directed porters

to rush the baggage to the ship and tipped them extra to make sure it got to the correct cabin.

Piper was still comforting her dog in a pouty baby language.

"I'm sorry. But if we don't hurry, we won't make it onto the ship." Carly gestured toward the customs desk.

"Oh, but I have to say goodbye to my little Pootsie darling." She held the dog up and nuzzled her face into the dog's neck. "Bye-bye, baby," she crooned. "Mommy has to go now. These mean ol' cruise people won't let me bring you. I'm going to miss you, yes I am." She smooched on the dog a couple more times, and hugged it to her breasts.

"I'm sorry, Piper, but they still need to check your passport, and if we don't hurry the ship will sail without us."

The tall, slim model gave a disgusted huff, gently handed the yapping dog to the assistant and stalked away.

With a barely aborted eye roll, Carly turned to greet her Average Joe. She blinked at the impossibly sculpted chest and massive biceps outlined by a tight black T-shirt. Average? There was nothing average about this man. His entry photo should've prepared her. But a five-by-seven glossy was no match for the living, breathing man in front of her.

In her stocking feet she was five-nine. With her heels, she reached six feet. And she still had to look up to meet his gaze. Warm brown eyes and shaggy black hair and that scruffy beard. She detested facial hair on a man. But standing this close to all that heat and muscle brought out something in her so raw, so primal that she had to catch her breath.

He cleared his throat and hefted a duffel bag higher on his broad shoulder. "Hiya."

"Mr. Te—Joe, I'm Carly Pendleton." She offered her right hand and he grabbed it hard, as if he didn't realize his own strength. "We spoke on the phone Saturday."

He nodded, stilled, and frowned. "Pendleton?"

"Yes." Resentment smoldered in her veins as it always did at this point in an introduction. "I'm his daughter. Does it matter?"

Holding on to her hand, his gaze scanned her body—down her legs and back up to meet her eyes. Then he flashed white teeth in a salacious smile. "Not a bit."

The smile hit her like a gale-force wind. His palm was rough and hot. Yes, she'd been right about the heat.

Pushing away the thought, she dropped her hand and stepped back, half turning away from him. "If you'll follow Piper to the customs desk, please?" She gestured toward the uniformed guards and the metal detector.

"Yes, ma'am." As he moved past her, a subtle scent wafted by. She closed her eyes and inhaled. Mmm. She had a nose for colognes and his was not by any designer she recognized. The fragrance was something old-fashioned. Uniquely masculine. And incredibly attractive.

"You all right?"

Joe's deep rumble startled her. Carly opened her eyes and met his gaze. He stared at her, the intensity in his dark brown eyes making her flinch. Her face warmed. Her throat tightened.

Great. Did she have *no* control over her body? She

pasted on a smile and nodded. "Just dandy." She brought her clipboard up and pretended to scrutinize page after page until Average Joe stepped up to hand his passport to the customs agent.

Dandy? She could kick herself. She'd graduated summa cum laude, for Pete's sake. And all she could come up with was dandy? Geez. This was going to be a long five days.

2

"STOP RIGHT THERE." Joe grabbed the wrist of the man trying to smear something on his eye.

The guy's lips flattened. He shoved his free hand on his hip, threw his head back and called out, "Ms. Pendleton!" in a high voice.

Joe searched the crowded suite for his nemesis. The place was a circus this morning. Though he had to admit, the accommodations were nice. This suite was a mirror image of his.

Last night he'd slept better than he expected. The shower head was too low, but that was par for him. The king-size bed had been comfortable, there was a sofa and a table with seating for two and the cabin even had a balcony.

But he'd barely gotten himself a cup of coffee this morning before someone had knocked on his door to escort him here. He'd been dragged to a chair in front of a lighted mirror and a woman started trying to cut his hair.

There had to be at least a dozen people in this cabin. Still, he easily found Carly Pendleton. She was the type to stand out in a crowd. Tall and slim, but she had curves in all the right places. Her skirt and blouse hugged her figure as if they'd been made for her. Which, come to think of it, they probably had. And her long, thick brunette hair had not a strand out of place, even at seven in the morning.

But her best feature was her eyes. They were the color of arctic ice. A light blue so vivid they could capture a man's gaze and freeze him where he stood, make him her prisoner until she deigned to set him free.

He shivered just thinking about being trapped in her frigid world. A man could get frostbite.

At the call of her name, Ms. Pendleton glanced over at the makeup guy, took another moment to nod and shake her head at a selection of clothing a woman held, and then walked over.

Just watching her walk riveted Joe's attention. The way she held her shoulders back and her chin slightly lifted, as if she was noble-born. She'd probably attended one of those fancy boarding schools. Surely, her father would've been able to afford it.

The only thing he remembered about her father's investment scandal was that his wife had claimed complete innocence of his scheme. The fact that the crook had a kid had barely registered.

"What is it, Christoph?"

"The *gentleman* won't let me apply liner to his eyes."

She trained those icy blues on him. "Joe, I realize it seems emasculating, but the sunlight and the camera will wash out your eyes without a little liner. Surely you're confident enough in your masculinity to allow a tiny bit of makeup?"

Oh, well, if she was going to challenge his masculinity... He folded his arms. "No."

Irritation sparked in her eyes. Hmm, the ice queen heated up. This could be fun.

She straightened her shoulders and folded her arms, too. His attention fixed on the outline of her lace bra through her thin silk blouse.

"Mr. Tedesco."

He imagined her only in delicate lacy lingerie, some sheer stockings and those ridiculously high heels of hers. Barely cutting off a groan, he scanned the room for a pitcher of water. His throat was dry.

"Mr. Tedesco? I already have one diva to deal with and she hasn't even deigned to show up yet." She tapped him on the shoulder. "Joe! Are you listening?"

"What?" He pulled his mind back from the beginnings of a sensual daydream. Noticed the bottle of water on the table beside him and grabbed it.

"I was saying that the liner won't be at all noticeable in the final version of the photo."

He twisted the cap off, gulped a few swallows and dried his lips on his sleeve. "In that case..." He leaned forward and she leaned in, too. "It's still no."

She jerked back, her eyes flared, anger spitting. Her perfectly shaped lips pinched. Her chest rose as she inhaled deeply. Then her face relaxed and she gave him a saccharine sweet smile. "Fine. We wouldn't want your Man Card revoked, now would we?" She trained her eyes on the makeup guy. "Christoph, just a light dusting of powder on the nose so he doesn't shine like Rudolph."

Her gaze zapped back to Joe. "Unless you're too manly for that?"

He grinned. "That's fine." No woman had ever talked to him this way before. Was this how all Manhattan women were? He'd lived in Brooklyn all his life, and the only women he hung around had known him since elementary school. To them he was Little Joey, the high school football hero.

"Thank you *so* much. Is there anything else I should obtain your permission on before I resume directing *my* photo shoot?"

He chuckled. "I'll let you know."

Her fake smile disappeared. "Tony," she called to a young man fiddling with some photo equipment. "Make sure the lighting on our Average Joe is filtered so he doesn't wash out." Then she spun on her heels and stalked back to the other side of the room.

She had the temper of a back-alley dog. And he had a feeling her bite was worse than her bark.

"No, that's not working." Carly heaved a sigh and shook her head. Honestly, she didn't know which one was worse, the high maintenance supermodel or the infuriatingly bullheaded contest winner. It didn't help that her stomach was churning and her head felt as if someone had jammed an ice pick in her temples. Didn't everyone else feel the ship listing from side to side?

She steeled herself to approach the couple. Piper must be handled with kid gloves. And Joe, well, Carly had to fight to keep her mind on business when she went near the guy.

"Piper, you're looking just gorgeous with the turquoise water behind you. Really brings out your eyes." They'd positioned the deck chairs against the railing and the Caribbean Sea sparkled in the warm sun. There was a tang of salt in the humid air. Humph. Carly would take New York cab exhaust any day.

Piper merely rolled said eyes. "You need to hurry this up. I'm tired and bored. And thirsty. Someone bring me a Bloody Mary."

Carly clenched her teeth and bit back what she wanted to say. "Yes, I'll get that ordered right away, but if I could just ask you to try to look more interested in Joe, for just a few moments?"

Piper raised a delicate brow that got lost in the fringe of her bangs. "I am."

"Yes, well, maybe a little more, please? And Joe." Carly focused her attention on his right shoulder. "When you're turned facing Piper in the deck chair, just turn from your waist, not your legs. Leave your legs facing forward please."

"Like this?" The man spread his knees and, whether intentionally or not, he seemed to flex his thigh muscles.

Now she was staring and Carly felt her face heat. She spun away, pretending to check the position of the sun.

When she could face him once more, she studied his shoulder again. "Yes, but you have to be turned toward Piper from the waist up." She cupped his shoulders to swivel his upper body. Her hands met rigid muscle beneath the starched cotton dress shirt. Heat radiated from him, scorching her palms. And there was that scent again. His cologne or shampoo, whatever it was made her knees weak. Or maybe that was just part of the seasickness.

"Not that I care, but you're wrinkling the Armani here," Joe said in a low tone.

Carly blinked, saw that her hands were gripping his arms, lifted them off and stepped away. "It's Hilfiger," she mumbled.

One side of his mouth crooked up in a smirk. But he laid his arm along the back of Piper's deck chair and turned from the waist exactly as Carly had asked.

Impressed, she headed for the camera to check the frame and, as she looked through the lens, Joe lifted his other hand to cup Piper's cheek and turn her to face him. He said something and flashed that dazzling smile and Piper actually smiled back.

Carly straightened and motioned for the photographer to step in and snap the picture. What had Joe said to Piper? As the camera snapped away, he spoke to the model again and her expression turned sultry, her eyes half-lidded. She stared at Joe as if she were about to rip his clothes off. Unbelievable.

Carly gaped as the two models spoke in whispered tones, their heads moving toward each other, their lips almost touching. The cameraman clicked pictures from every angle, encouraging them. Piper unbuttoned Joe's shirt and slipped a hand inside, rubbing her fingers over his chest. Then her hand dropped to his thigh, over his denim shorts, but inching her way to—

"That's great!" Carly yelled. "Thank you, everyone."

She moved forward to stand before Piper, who'd, thankfully, removed her hand from Joe's thigh, even if she did radiate annoyance.

Too bad. Carly's headache had worsened and she wasn't in the mood to indulge the diva. She bent from the waist to scrutinize Piper's face. "We're done for today, but be sure to get a good night's sleep. We have an early morning shoot and there's only so much makeup can do for dark circles."

Piper gasped, and then narrowed those light green eyes to glare at Carly. "If I have dark circles it's because the cabin you put me in is deplorable! I can't sleep there. You'll have to find me something larger. On a higher deck. And while you're at it—"

"I'm afraid there are no other rooms larger than what you have." Carly clenched her fists around her clipboard. "I can look into seeing if there are any cabins available on a higher deck, but—"

"Then do it!" The prima donna pushed up out of the deck chair and stomped off in a high-heeled huff.

Joe got to his feet. A smitten half grin quirked his lips as he watched Piper walk away, her pert little butt perfectly displayed in the white designer short-shorts. Of course Joe *would* be attracted to Ms. Exotic.

Carly spun to face her lighting and camera crew. "Tomorrow we dock in Grand Turk at 7:00 a.m. Be ready to disembark at 6:45. I've reserved a chartered plane and want to head to the Caicos Islands. Take whatever special equipment you might need for shooting outdoors, and inside a cave. We have to be back on the ship by 7:00 p.m., and Thursday we disembark at Half Moon

Cay. I want shots on the white sandy beaches there, Friday we'll only shoot for a few hours in Nassau. It's all on your itinerary I handed out yesterday after the safety drill. Any questions?"

In the silence of shaking heads she turned back around and saw Joe was fingering a tiny slip of paper. Was that Piper's room number? Was he going to meet her there tonight? Or…had they slept together already?

Ignoring the sharp pinch in her stomach, she gave her attention to the crew disassembling the photo equipment. But she felt Joe's presence behind her. She turned to face him. "My recommendation pertains to you, too, Mr. Tedesco."

"Recommendation?" His grin had disappeared and his brows rose. His chest exposed by the unbuttoned shirt was taut and tanned with a light dusting of hair.

Carly diverted her gaze to his face. "Yes. To get a good night's sleep. I can't have my Sexiest Average Joe showing up tomorrow looking haggard and unkempt."

He scowled and took a step closer to her. "Unkempt?"

His bronze skin gleamed in the sunlight that also played in his breeze-ruffled black hair. She remembered he was a fireman and probably worked out to maintain his muscular physique. His shoulders blocked her view of anything but him, and her knees wanted to buckle. Her knees? Weak? Over a man she barely knew? What was she, some pathetic romance-novel heroine? It was just that she hadn't eaten today yet. She probably had low blood sugar. And with her height, she was unaccustomed to men looming over her. He was invading her personal space. So, naturally his overwhelming frame felt…well, overwhelming.

"Unkempt. It means disheveled, messy, slovenly."

He folded his arms and his biceps bulged. "I know what it means." His mouth was a grim line. He looked irritated.

"Good. Then perhaps whatever you're planning for tonight can be postponed until I've finished my photo shoot."

His face crinkled up in a confused expression. "What do you think I have planned for tonight?"

"You don't have to pretend with me. I realize she's beautiful and glamorous. What guy could resist that? But until—"

"Look, lady." He dropped his arms to place his hands low on his hips and half turned away. Then he leaned toward her. "First of all, if I wanted her, I wouldn't be deterred by an uptight, bossy, arrogant—" he clamped his mouth shut "—woman," he finished between his teeth.

Carly's temper flared. "Uptight? Just because I don't lose control and crawl all over you like Ms. Supermodel?"

He raised his brows and smiled. "So, you *want* to crawl all over me?"

All that raw sex appeal wrapped in a killer grin. Despite her irritation, she pictured herself in his lap, their mouths exploring one another, her hands all over his six feet four inches of gleaming muscles. The air whooshed from her lungs. She couldn't breathe. She was horrified. Mortified. "No!" She dragged in a breath. "I mean, that is not at all what I was saying." She clamped her mouth shut and folded her arms in front of her. "Just…" She waved a hand in his direction. "Be on time tomorrow." She stalked away. And heard him chuckle behind her.

The thought of him in Piper's bed, rolling around in the sheets with her, naked, made Carly's chest feel hollow. But…maybe she'd get the best photos of them if they *were* sleeping together? Just like a few moments ago, they'd been cooing at each other like lovebirds and the results had been fantastic.

So, let them have at it, what did she care? Besides, Joe was practically an employee. How awkward would a one-night stand be with him when they had to work together the next few days?

And maybe if she kept repeating all those excuses to herself, she could keep from throwing herself at him and ripping his clothes off.…

She knew what her problem was. It'd been a long time since Reese had moved out. She just missed being touched. Missed a warm body beside her at night.

But losing Reese had been inevitable. She should never have moved in with him. And she didn't blame him for leaving. He hadn't understood her drive to succeed. He'd complained about her long hours at the apparel factory, and then coming home at night to work on her blog.

Now, her years of sacrifice had paid off with this remarkable opportunity from *Modiste*. And she wasn't going to let anything ruin it. The success of her blog depended on this photo shoot. And the success of this photo shoot depended on making her troublesome supermodel happy.

She'd thought that when *Modiste* hired Piper to pose with her contest winner, the controversial model might draw more entries and consequently more followers, but now she wasn't sure Piper was worth it. The woman was petulant, whiny and demanding. She'd shown up over an hour late this morning with no excuse or apology.

But the photos they'd taken of her and Joe were golden. Carly could picture them on the cover of *Modiste* magazine. If everything worked out as she hoped, maybe she could get the editor at *Modiste* to agree to sponsor a Sexiest Average Jane contest next season. And with her *Carly's Couture* blog linked to the best-selling magazine she was insured success. Then, maybe the Pendleton name would come to be associated with something other than heartless greed.

But first she had to see the captain about a vacant cabin on a higher deck.

3

PIPER SPUN ON the dance floor, gyrating her hips to the beat of the deafening rock music. With her eyes closed, she lost herself in the thumping bass and flashing lights. The crowds of young, carefree people dancing all around her were her sanctuary.

She loved nightclubs. She loved champagne and loud music and having men fall all over themselves to be with her. And the freedom to tell them to get lost. Ahhh, the freedom. She'd missed that in rehab.

Thank the gods her agent had gotten her out of that place! Her counselor had wanted to discuss the past. But Piper the Supermodel had no past. Anju Rajaraman was dead. She'd died eight years ago in the slums of Calcutta. She was Piper now. And Piper would never go back to being that starving, powerless little girl.

Why was she thinking of those days? She was here to have fun.

She lifted her arms above her head and spun again, checking out the men in the cruise ship's nightclub.

Her gaze strayed to the adjoining piano bar and landed on the tall, dark and sexy hunk of man she'd posed with all day. He'd told her that Carly was wrong. That her eyes made the turquoise water seem dull in comparison. Mmm, yes, he was interesting.

Running her hands through her hair, she danced her way over to the glass door and entered the quieter room. A few passengers were scattered around intimate little tables. Joe sat at one of them, nursing a tumbler of amber-colored liquid.

"Come dance with me?"

He looked up from his glass into her eyes, glanced over at the nightclub dance floor, and then met her gaze again with a grimace. "Not really my thing."

Piper pouted, but took the other chair, crossing her legs and leaning her elbows on the table. The skimpy, sparkly dress had a draped bodice that showed off her cleavage when she bent over. She watched his gaze take in the view. "Buy me a drink?"

His eyes rose to her face again. "Sure." He motioned to the waitress. "What'll you have?"

"Appletini," she ordered when the waitress appeared. After she left, Piper sat back and lifted her hair off the back of her neck. "So, a New York firefighter, huh?"

He nodded. "Brooklyn."

"And you go around saving lives?"

He shrugged. "A few."

Humility? It must be an act. Men were never what they seemed. Eventually, he'd show his true stripes. Then she would shut him down. She leaned forward again and slid a finger up his sleeve. "Don't be so modest."

His gaze followed her fingers and then looked up into her eyes. "Uh…"

"Don't you want—"

He took her hand and moved it back to the table. "You're a beautiful woman, Piper, but—"

"Never mind. You think I would actually be with a fireman from…Brooklyn?" Grabbing her Appletini, she scooted her chair back, stood and returned to the nightclub. After she downed the drink in one swallow, she ordered another from the bar and then joined the crowd on the dance floor.

He'd turned her down? Then why had he flirted with her all day during the photo shoot? She hadn't noticed a wedding ring—as if that ever stopped a man.

Forget him. There were plenty more where he came from. It wasn't as if she ever enjoyed it anyway. Sometimes, it was simply a way to forget, if just for a little while….

And here she was thinking of the past again. That was the counselor's fault. *Think only of this moment, Piper.*

This moment was all she had.

JOE WATCHED PIPER flounce off in her high heels and short dress, her hips swaying dramatically. Everyone in the bar had their cell phones out snapping her picture.

Yeah, that woman was Drama with a capital *D*. Between his job and family, he had enough of that in his life. Bad enough he had to have his photo taken with her splashed all over a national magazine. If he became her boy toy for the cruise's duration and someone snapped a picture on their cell…

The guys would rib him endlessly over that, but Joe could do without the fifteen minutes of fame. What he wanted was quiet. Calm. Normal.

"There you are." Carly appeared at his table. "Christoph said he saw you in here."

Whoa. She wore a slinky, strapless navy gown that looked as though it would be right at home sauntering down the red carpet. Cleavage peeking out and all. He swallowed. "Wow."

Carly looked down, examining herself with a perplexed expression on her face. "Oh, I dined with the captain tonight. You received an invitation."

"Yeah, I don't do monkey suits." Although if he'd known Carly would be there looking like this…

"Listen, Joe. I need…a favor."

Joe straightened in his chair, pulled the empty one out for her. "Have a seat."

"Thanks." She sat, closed her eyes and massaged her temples.

Joe took the opportunity to study her. She was the one who looked haggard. Dark circles under her eyes were prominent, and she seemed weighted by exhaustion. She was more fun when she was biting his head off. This more vulnerable Carly threw him off balance, made him want to protect her.

When the waitress came over, Carly ordered water and then pulled a tiny golden pill case from a little purse that matched the dress.

"Are you all right?"

"I'm fine." She opened the case and shook out two pills. "I think I spent too much time in my cabin staring at my laptop this afternoon. It's just a bit of mal de mer."

Joe recognized the pills to combat motion sickness. Had she not had time to relax since the photo shoot this morning? That was no way to live.

"That's seasickness."

This assuming he was ignorant was getting annoying. "Yeah, I gathered that. What can I do for you?"

"I—" The waitress set a cold bottle of water down along with an empty glass and Carly popped the pills into her mouth and chased them down with the water. Her shoulders sagged and she released a breath. Then, as if gathering her strength, she drew in a deep breath, sat up straight, and met his gaze. "I need you to switch cabins with Piper."

Joe blinked. That was it? "No problem."

Her eyes widened and her mouth dropped open. "Really? You don't mind? It's just that your cabin is on a higher deck than mine and there aren't any other suites avail—"

"It's fine."

She slumped against the back of the chair. "Thank you. You have no idea…I talked to the cruise director at dinner and he said he could have the stewards move your things. If you'll give me your key card, I'll go get Piper's." She frowned and finally looked at him again.

Pulling his card from his pocket, he nodded toward the nightclub. "She's next door dancing."

Carly's gaze followed his. "I'll be right back." Her

mouth pursed in grim determination as she took his key card.

Joe watched her walk away, appreciating the curve of her figure outlined by the fitted gown. When she approached the supermodel in the middle of the dance floor, he could practically read the conversation from their gestures and facial expressions.

Piper pulled a card from her tiny shoulder-strapped purse and exchanged it for the one Carly gave her, but not before making some snarky remark. Carly stiffened, but kept her mouth closed. She dropped the card in her purse, spun and headed back toward him.

Joe knocked back the rest of his whiskey and got to his feet as she returned. "Okay, all I need to do now is call the cruise director. At dinner, he said he could change the cabins' occupancy information and all the key cards have *Modiste's* credit information, so that doesn't change." She pulled the key card from her purse and dropped it in his waiting hand. Her brows were knitted in pain and she actually swayed.

He caught her, straightened her. "How about I walk you back to your cabin."

She leaned into him, clutching his shoulder. So soft in his arms. Heat and need flared inside him. He closed his eyes as blood surged southward, leaving him light-headed, and hard. She shivered, inhaled a ragged breath, her pale blue eyes peering at him with…fear? Confusion? Then they iced over. She pulled out of his grip, stepped back. "No. I'll be fine."

He stuck his hands in his pants pockets, shoving the key card deep. "Suit yourself."

"But." She reached out and grasped his arm. "Thank you." Then she dropped her hand and left, her tough, no-nonsense stride contradicting the claim of seasickness.

"Hey." He strode after her.

She stopped and turned.

"What's my new cabin number?"

"Forty-eight seventy-t— No!" She squeezed her eyes closed and shook her head. "I'm sorry. Piper's is—" She bit her bottom lip, then her face cleared and she smiled. "Forty-two seventy-eight." With a wave of her hand she was striding out the door again.

Joe stood there giving himself a moment to recover from the whiplash to his libido. He could've sworn she'd felt whatever had sparked between them, too. But, it was just as well. Even if she was the most interesting woman he'd met in too long to remember. And more challenging than any woman he ever dealt with. She was too uptight. Too bossy. Too…whatever.

Forget about it! He was on a cruise ship with round the clock entertainment. When would he ever get this kind of chance again? He made his way to the casino, found a stool in front of a one-armed bandit and ordered a couple more drinks while he fed it quarters.

Bleary-eyed and out of coins, he checked his cell. 1:37 a.m. He'd better head to bed. Feeling just buzzed enough to take the edge off his sexual frustrations, he stood and made his way to the elevator. But once he got in the elevator and punched his old deck number he re-membered he'd switched rooms with the diva and—he couldn't remember what his new room number was. If he hadn't been so distracted by sexy Carly and her sweet sexy curves and those ice-blue eyes…

He shook his head to clear it and remembered. Forty-seven eighty-two. He punched the button for the fourth deck and when the elevator let him out he walked down the long hall suddenly exhausted and dizzy. Perhaps he had a bit of mal de mer, too.

Ahh, here was forty-eight seventy-two. The key card clicked and the door opened with ease. He let out a relieved breath he wouldn't have to call someone for help and look like an idiot.

The room was pitch-dark, but he didn't want to bother to switch on the big overhead light. Man, he was more tired than he'd realized. He flipped on the tiny light in the closet.

The cabin didn't have a balcony as he'd expected Piper's would have, but he didn't care. The king-size bed awaited. He shucked his jeans, crawled onto the soft mattress, and was asleep as soon as his head hit the pillow.

Still, even in his dreams he couldn't get Carly out of his mind. Her spicy scent filled his senses and he felt her soft breasts pushing against his back. In his dream he turned over and wrapped his arms around her hot body. It seemed so real that he could've sworn he could feel the silky material of her nightgown catch on the calluses of his palms. He nuzzled into a sweetly soft neck, pushed his rigid erection against her stomach and heard her moan.

He stilled. Forced his heavy lids to open. And looked right into Carly's wide-open eyes.

And then she screamed.

4

CARLY SHOVED OUT of Joe's arms and scrambled off the bed. "What are you doing here? How'd you get in my room?"

"*Your* room?" Joe rose up on one elbow and ran a hand through his hair, all the while his gaze fixated on her...

She followed *where* he was staring. She wore only her thong underwear and a cami. And the underwear didn't hide much. She snatched the comforter off the bed and draped it around her. "Yes, my room. Do you honestly think *I'd* sneak into your room and crawl into your bed?"

He sat up, looking around the room. The sheet fell down to his waist and Carly didn't even try not to gape. Taut, defined muscles and dark hair that tapered to a line down past his belly button. Wow, even his belly button was sexy. He threw back the sheet and Carly spun to avert her gaze. From the corner of her eye she saw him swing his legs over the edge of the mattress on his side, his back to her. "If this is *your* room, then why did *my* key work?"

Her mind couldn't focus. This *was* her room, wasn't it? She didn't remember using her key… The medication must have really knocked her out. She hadn't slept so deeply in ages. But now her memory seemed to be missing parts of last night. She recalled getting Joe and Piper to switch cabins. Feeling dizzy again in the elevator and barely making it to her room, and—*Oh!*

She spun back to face him and snapped her fingers. "The steward!" *Aha.* "I didn't have to use my key because the steward was in here turning down my bed when I—"

Joe had stood and moved around the bed, searching the floor, wearing black boxer briefs that hugged him nice and snug.

She swallowed. Out of breath all of a sudden. "—got here," she finished lamely.

Shaking his head, he bent over and grabbed his pants off the floor. "I used the key you gave me to get in. This is the room number you told me was mine. So, if this isn't my cabin, then it's your fault I'm in here." He shoved his legs—very long, very brawny legs—into the pants and yanked them up.

Carly blinked, trying to remember. Could she have given him her key?

Holding the bottom of the comforter up like the train of a long gown, she marched to the table, grabbed her bag and dug around for her key. By the time she found it and got to the door, Joe was already there, his key pulled from his pocket. He was so close his dark brown eyes looked like pools of rich, molten fudge. He smelled of sleepy linen and the faintest hint of masculine sweat. Oh, why hadn't he put on his shirt? She realized she was staring at him.

"If my key works you're going to owe me," he said.

She snapped back. "Owe you what?" She didn't owe him a thing. If he thought he could—

"Well, I was going for an apology, but if you had something else in mind…" He raised a brow and gave her a slow, suggestive smile.

Ignoring the bare chest in front of her, Carly pursed her lips. "Just try your key."

"And if it doesn't work are you going to leave me standing out in the hall the rest of the night?"

"Not so sure about your key, now, huh?"

His smile dropped and his eyes narrowed. "Fine." He opened the door, stepped outside and Carly closed the door in his face.

A second later she heard the click of a key swiping, the handle turned and the door shoved open. Joe stepped inside wearing a smug expression. "So, what do you bet *your* key opens Piper's room?"

Oh, no. What had she done? She stared at the key in her hand. He probably thought she'd purposely given him her key and room number. That this was all a ploy to get him. Did he think that she was so desperate for sex, or for him in particular? She'd never. She squeezed her eyes closed, too embarrassed to look at him.

"Hey, everybody makes mistakes." His rough fingers cupped her chin and lifted her face.

She made herself open her eyes and meet his gaze. "I swear, I didn't—"

"I know." The fingers of his other hand caressed her cheek. He lowered his head and gently touched his lips to hers.

And that was all it took. She opened her mouth and took the kiss deep, her lips as desperate and as needy as she'd convinced herself she wasn't minutes ago. She pressed him to her, wrapping her arms around his neck, running her hands over his taut shoulders and fingering the curls at the base of his neck.

With a low growl he took control of the kiss, teasing her with his tongue. His arms tightened around her waist. He lifted her, and she hooked a leg around his hip as he walked them to the bed. The comforter slipped down to her hips and he broke the kiss, grinned and laid her on the mattress.

Joe's eyes flared as he stared at her body. Feeling her feminine power, Carly lay back on her elbows and raised one knee, then let it drop.

She watched as his Adam's apple bobbed when he swallowed. He raised a brow, unzipped his pants and got rid of them, along with his underwear.

Her breath caught. He was magnificent. How was this guy still single? Wait. Maybe he had a girlfriend.

He lowered himself over her, bracing himself with his hands. With one knee bent between her thighs, he nuzzled into her neck, nibbling the sensitive skin from below her ear to her shoulder.

Carly closed her eyes, shivering at the feel of his lips exploring, moving down her collarbone… What had she been about to ask him? Something about too good to be true… A girlfriend. She snapped her eyes open and flattened her palms on his chest.

He raised his head and frowned. "What's wrong?"

"You have a fiancée?"

"Hell, no."

"A girlfriend?"

His face contorted in disgust. "I wouldn't be here, doing this with you if I did." He shoved off the bed and bent to pull up his pants.

Carly scooted forward to the edge and covered his hands as he was about to zip up. "Wait."

"I think the mood has passed, don't you?"

"It's just that generally when something seems too good to be true, it's because it is."

He scoffed. "And what about me seems too good?"

"Well, you did just win *Modiste's* sexiest Average Joe." She let go of his hands and ran her palms over his chest, reveling in the wall of muscle, and large flat nipples. "You have to admit you're exceptionally attractive."

Now he caught her hands. "I know I don't exactly scare women away."

"Come on!" She looked up into his eyes, saw the disbelief there. "You really didn't enter our contest yourself, did you?"

"Does it matter as long as I'm here?"

She shook her head. "Not a bit."

He cupped her face, his fingers combing back her hair. "Then, where were we?" He bent and captured her mouth and Carly assumed it was a rhetorical question.

She couldn't get enough of his mouth moving over hers, his tongue playing with hers. She writhed beneath him when he caught her breast in his palm, kneading and caressing it until the nipple became a sensitive peak. His lips deserted her mouth and left a hot, moist trail down her jaw and neck to the top of her breast. He tugged the thin strap of her cami down until he could capture her nipple and draw on it deeply.

Shifting his weight to her side, he teased her nipple as the fingers of his other hand slid down her hip and slipped under her thong.

She moaned, bucking in time to his intimate touch. The exquisite pressure was building inside her.

The orgasm hit her hard and fast and she cried out. A fog of pleasure enveloped her. She couldn't move. Couldn't quite believe this was happening. That she'd let this happen. She was vaguely aware he was pressing tiny kisses around her breast, still stroking her sensitized core. He was skilled, all right. But it was more than that. More than just his unbelievable physique and charming smile. She'd met plenty of good-looking guys. But Joe seemed—the word sounded silly—but… he seemed sincere.

"Well, my job is done here." Joe started to remove his hand and sit up.

Her eyes snapped open and she caught his wrist. "What?"

He grinned and chuckled. "Just wanted to see if you were still with me."

With a growl, she shoved his chest until he lay on his back. She climbed over him, straddling his knees, unzipped his pants and encircled his cock. "Oh, I'm with you, all right." She bent and took him in her mouth.

Behaving like this was so unlike her. She didn't usually do playful in bed. This wild, intense response to Joe was mad. She'd probably regret it.

But not tonight.

He moaned and whispered her name. Thus encouraged, she put all her effort into driving him crazy. She took him deep and then teased him with her tongue, then deep again. He cursed and lifted his hips, tangling his fingers in her hair.

When she raised her gaze to watch him, his eyes were squeezed closed, his head thrown back and she could see a vein or two enlarged in his neck. She grinned. Turnabout was fair play. She swirled her tongue around the head once more before he urged her to stop.

"Okay, I give." His chest rose and fell in heavy breaths, but his mouth was turned up in a lopsided smile. "Uncle. You win."

With a seductive smile Carly pulled the cami over her head and tossed it to the floor. His gaze dropped to her breasts and he reached up to cup them in his large callused hands. His touch was so sensual, the look in his eyes admiring. She hadn't felt desirable in so long.

She wanted him inside her.

She kneeled in order to drag her thong down and off, but she lost her balance, flailed awkwardly and fell onto him.

"Whoa!" He caught her and rolled her to her back, smiling. "You aren't as graceful as you pretend."

Carly clamped a hand over her eyes. This was ridiculous. What was wrong with her? She was twenty-eight, not eighteen. And even at eighteen she hadn't fumbled sex as badly as she was tonight. First she'd insulted his fidelity, now this. "Maybe this wasn't such a good idea."

The aggravating man chuckled more. "If it helps, I like you better this way." She felt him tug her thong down to her ankles and off. Then, as she lifted her fingers away from her eyes, his hand traced a path up her leg, sending shivers along her skin.

Wait. She rose to her elbows and gripped his wrist. "So, you're saying you didn't like me before?"

"I didn't say that. But maybe I like you a little more this way."

"What way?"

"Relaxed. With your guard down."

She let out a relieved breath. Relieved? Since when had she ever worried about being liked? Oh, who cared? He was caressing her hip, her stomach, and he'd leaned over to close his lips around one nipple, then moved his hand slowly down.

Her breathing faltered as he delved between her thighs with the exact right amount of pressure and an exquisite sense of timing. Much more of this and she'd be a goner for a second time. But she wanted him inside her when she came again. "Joe." Was that her voice all husky and trembling?

"Hmm?" he answered around nibbling her other nipple, his unshaven jaw tickling her breast.

She gripped his shoulders. "Stop teasing me."

He narrowed his eyes, but he was smiling. "Really? You have to boss me around even now?"

Boss him around? Is that how he saw her? She wasn't demanding. She was begging. She was coming apart in his arms.

With a sigh, he rolled above her, pushed his erection against her hip and took possession of her mouth. She made approving noises, wrapped her arms around his neck, and hooked a leg over his thigh. "I'm not bossy I just know what I like."

He chuckled against her lips and then pulled back long enough to grab a condom from his pocket before getting rid of his pants completely. "And this is what you like?"

She quirked a brow. "Yes, please."

The way he looked at her, it was as if he knew how lonely she was, how scared she was to admit she needed someone. His gaze seemed to penetrate the layer of bravado she'd built around herself. As if he could see the real Carly.

"All right." In a fluid motion he rolled on protection and fitted himself to her entrance. Then, with a satisfied groan he was where she wanted him. Needed him.

She gasped at the feel of him inside her. His head dropped to her neck as he began moving, thrusting at an angle and in a rhythm that made her say wicked things. She wasn't usually verbal in her lovemaking, but she found herself murmuring, "Yes. Oh, yes. Oh, Joe," over and over again.

The more she encouraged him, the faster and harder he thrust, building to a frenzy of pleasure. "Please." Winding her fingers into his silky black hair, she nipped at his ear, as everything spun out of control. She cried out, clutching his back at the same time he froze above her. His muscles contracted beneath her hands as he made a low growling sound deep in his throat and pumped his hips one last time.

Neither of them moved for several minutes. She was still reveling in the best sex of her life. He was breathing heavily above her, but careful to keep his weight on his elbows. She almost wanted to pull him down and tell him it was okay, to relax, to touch his skin to hers, but that seemed too intimate. Too…emotional. And yet, she felt a niggling sense of happiness. As if things weren't as dire as she'd always believed they were. She smiled and rubbed his back and he moaned and moved to her side. Air blew over her sweat-moistened skin and cooled her.

He rolled to his back and ran a hand through his hair. "Wow."

"Yeah." There. That sounded okay, didn't it? Not too enthusiastic. She wasn't gushing any more than he was.

But she wanted to. She wanted to roll over and press kisses all over his sexy, strong chest. How silly was that? She needed to get herself back under control. She should get up and head to the bathroom and tell him to find his own room now. And not to expect that this was going to happen again. Because it wasn't. It couldn't.

She had a photo shoot to supervise. This was the most important career opportunity of her life. If she blew this there wouldn't be another. And Joe was as vital to her success. Not to mention she needed to maintain a professional relationship with him. Which meant she needed to make sure he understood tonight had been a one-off. Never again.

He rolled to face her, cupped her face in his hands and planted a kiss that promised he wasn't anywhere near done. "Let's do that again."

She blinked and looked into his eyes, glinting with anticipation. "Okay."

5

AND TO THINK he hadn't wanted to come on this cruise.

Joe stepped out of the taxi and scanned the scene before him. Whoa. No wonder the magazine had gone to so much trouble to get them to North Caicos Island. From Grand Turk they'd had to take a chartered plane to Providenciales and from there they'd had to hire half a dozen taxis to drive to this island.

But Joe had to admit it was worth it. This was paradise. They were on a high bluff overlooking a deserted beach. The palm trees and foliage lining the crescent-shaped beach looked like CGI for a movie. Turquoise water, gentle waves and smooth white sand. Give him a cold beer and he'd be in heaven.

Then Joe saw Carly emerge from a taxi pulling up behind his and revised that thought. Carly in his arms again would be his version of heaven.

She was wearing white capris and a brightly colored shirt cinched by a wide white belt. She wore strappy heels, of course, and all the perfect accessories. Her hair was up, with wispy tendrils falling loose around her face and down her neck. She should be posing for the magazine herself, she was always so perfectly put together.

Well, not always. Joe smiled, remembering her, just a few hours earlier, lying beside him gloriously naked, her arm bent holding her head in one hand, her knee bent in a provocative pose. Her skin had been damp with perspiration, her lips red and swollen from his kisses, and her eyes half-lidded in satisfaction. And despite the sated laziness his body had felt, he could've kept going if they hadn't had to be ready to disembark in less than an hour.

But there was always tonight.

He grinned as he caught her eye. So much for getting a good night's sleep, right? And if he had shown up "unkempt," whose fault was that?

Carly didn't return his smile. Her lips thinned and she spun to direct the lighting and camera crews to set up in front of the ruins of the main house up the path. Joe chuckled. She could pretend icy indifference all she wanted. He knew there was a fire burning in that woman that could scorch a guy if he didn't know how to handle the flames. Luckily, he was a trained professional. Although maybe with Carly, he'd need some extra practice....

"This heat is unbearable." Joe turned to see Piper stumble awkwardly from another taxi. She wore dark shades and a large floppy hat, and she started swatting madly at the mosquitoes buzzing about. "If I get bitten I'm going to sue someone."

Carly had warned everyone on the plane about the mosquitoes and handed out a supply of bug repellant. Piper ordered her makeup assistant to apply it on her while she'd been waiting for the taxis. "Oh, this heat is intolerable!" Piper fanned herself with her hand. "Where are we? It looks like the middle of nowhere. Where's the hotel? Is there not even a restroom? You!" She snapped her fingers at a poor assistant carrying cables and tripods down a dirt path. "Direct me to the nearest facilities."

"Uh…" The unlucky gofer looked at Joe with pleading eyes.

Joe sighed. "Maybe you can think of this as an adventure." He reached out to take her arm and lead her down the path. "The intrepid supermodel braving a primitive environment."

"What rubbish." Piper's scowl remained as she snatched her sunglasses off and gazed around her. For the first time, he really examined the woman. Or girl, really. She couldn't be more than twenty-two, twenty-three. She wore red short-shorts with a hot pink halter top. Her body was perfection. Full breasts and tiny waist, thin to the point of skeletal, taller than Carly. Her caramel skin and thick, straight black hair hinted at her exotic heritage.

"Piper. Joe." Carly strode toward them, a pile of clothes draped over one arm. "These are your outfits for the shoot." She led them down a worn path through dense foliage to a cornerstone with a two-story-tall chimney still standing. "There's a mostly intact stone building this way where you can change, Piper." She gestured to the right for Piper, and Joe to the left. "And another building this way for you, Joe."

Joe took the clothes she handed him and winced. Tall black boots. Tight black jeans. And a crisp white shirt with gold cuff links. All with famous labels.

What was he supposed to be? A designer-wearing pirate? All he needed was the eye patch and parrot. He gritted his teeth and remembered his agreement. Mumbling a curse under his breath he yanked his T-shirt off and began unbuttoning his shorts. Just get this over with.

When he'd finished dressing he headed for the sound of Carly's voice directing the crew. She'd set up the shoot at a half wall with the beach behind it. The stunning view behind these old ruins made for a great location. Carly really knew what she was doing. Joe paused to admire her.

Directing the cameraman and lighting crew, she wiped her temple with the back of her hand. She wasn't complaining about the heat or the bugs. She had ambition and wasn't afraid to work hard to get what she wanted.

He made his way to her side. "Where do you want me?" Though he'd meant the double entendre, he hadn't meant to startle her.

She jumped and swiveled to face him, glaring. Then her gaze lowered down his body, slowly. She made a funny little sound, not quite a whimper, and swallowed as her gaze traveled back up and stopped at his chest. She licked her lips and then reached up and began unbuttoning the shirt. All the way down to the waistband of the jeans. "There." Her voice was barely a whisper. She licked her lips and finally met his eyes. "Women are going to go crazy for this one."

Disappointment thudded in his chest. Was that all he was to her? A commodity to sell magazines? Wait. Of course he was. Why had he begun to think otherwise? Just because he'd felt a connection with her last night? She was tough, but feminine. Assertive, disciplined, goal-oriented. And he wanted to get to know her better. She obviously didn't share the sentiment. Hadn't he learned anything from the break up with Lydia?

"Where's Piper?" Carly sidestepped past him, heading in the direction of the ruins where she'd sent Piper to change. "Joe, go to Christoph for a little makeup, please?" she called over her shoulder.

Makeup. Great. But, hey. It beat having to deal with the diva. Joe didn't envy Carly tha—

"Joe!" Carly's terrified shriek had him racing toward her before he knew exactly where he was going. Was it a snake? Had she fallen down the cliff? His heart pounded double time picturing her injured, scared. He followed the path, rounded a corner and found her hunched over Piper, who was curled up in the corner of two crumbling walls, shaking, gasping for breath.

"She says she can't breathe," Carly offered.

He squatted and checked Piper's pulse. Rapid, erratic. Her pupils were dilated. Not good.

"Any other symptoms?"

Carly shook her head, shrugging.

Joe cupped Piper's face in his hands and spoke firmly. "Piper, look at me."

The girl flinched, but her eyes met his.

"Does anything hurt?"

"M-my chest hurts."

"Are you dizzy? Nauseated?"

She nodded.

"Were you bitten by anything?"

She shook her head. "I…don't know. Don't think so."

"Have you eaten today? Taken any drugs?"

She turned her head, closed her eyes.

He glanced at Carly. "We have a first-aid kit?"

She nodded.

"Get it. And some water. Hurry."

Carly got to her feet and took off at a sprint.

He turned his attention back to Piper. "Has this happened before?"

Between gasping for breaths she shook her head.

"Piper. Look at me." He put a finger beneath her chin. "I want you to raise your arms above your head and take as deep a breath as you can, slowly, and then let it out slowly. Can you do that?"

Her panicked eyes stared into his a moment, then she blinked and nodded. Her breathing was already slowing.

He shifted his weight to one knee and gently lifted her arms. "Breathe in."

She obeyed.

"Now breathe out."

She followed his instructions and he repeated the breathing commands. Then Carly returned with the kit and the water. After several gulps Piper seemed back to normal.

"Is she going to be all right?" Carly asked Joe.

"I'm fine now. It's this bloody heat."

He checked Piper's pulse again. Steady, only slightly fast. If his diagnosis was correct, she needed more than to cool off. "You should eat something."

Piper shoved him away and got to her feet. "If you really want to help, find me an air-conditioned building." She brushed dirt from her outfit, then grabbed her hat and sunglasses from the ground.

Joe took that as his cue to leave and headed back for the bluff. The witch was back to normal all right. Just because he was a trained paramedic didn't mean she had to listen to him.

"Joe," Carly called from behind him. He stopped and turned as she jogged up.

"Thank you."

"No problem." He nodded. "She going to continue the shoot?"

"I asked her to see how she feels after she rests for a while." She gestured down the path and he noticed she was carrying her high heels by the straps. "Piper insists it's the heat."

He raised his brows, highly doubting that was the problem. He remembered the way she'd gone all ashy-faced when he mentioned the word drugs and asked if she'd been drinking. With her reputation, who knew?

"What's that look about?" Carly scrutinized his face. "You don't believe her?"

He shook his head. "It's nothing."

She grabbed his arm before he could turn to go. "Wait. If there's something going on that will affect my photo shoot, I need to know."

Carly had a point. And her hand on his arm was like a cushioned vise. There was no tight grip, but it held him captive just the same. "Look, I'm not a medical doctor. This isn't an official diagnosis. But, you might want to talk to Piper about panic attacks."

"Panic attacks?" Hands on her hips, she spun from the waist to glance behind them, then faced front again. "I thought you were going to say something about drugs."

"Could be stress-induced from a busy schedule, combined with the heat. Find out if she's ever had an attack or received treatment for them before."

"Wow." She nodded, her expression still confused. "Okay, I'll talk to her and try to keep a closer eye on her." She pulled her sunglasses off, met his gaze and lifted her hand to his shoulder. "Really. Thank you."

Joe gazed at her hand, then into her eyes. She licked her lips and swallowed and Joe studied the movements. Without stopping to think, he cupped her cheek and lowered his head. She stepped closer and raised her chin. Their lips almost touched.

"I cannot do this now," Piper called, coming along the path. "I want to return to the ship."

Carly jumped back and gave her attention to placating her supermodel.

It was going to be a long day.

PIPER BARELY MANAGED to keep her mask of indifference in place until she reached the line of taxis waiting in the road. She ordered the taxi driver to go away, and then climbed into the backseat and slowly drew her knees up to her chin.

Nandan. He should be with her. If only she hadn't left him. Her brother had only been ten the last time she saw him.

Squeezing her eyes tight, she dug her nails into her palms. She heard her manager's—Mrs. Henderson's—clipped voice in her head. *Stop crying!*

She let out her breath on one last gulp. Then silence.

Mrs. Henderson had been right. Allowing herself to wallow in her emotions did not make her feel better. She felt worse. Weak. Foolish. And it solved nothing. She'd had private detectives searching for Nandan for more than five years. But it was as if he'd vanished from the earth.

The wind gusted in from the sea across the high bluff, blowing through the palm fronds. Seagulls squawked and other birds sang happy chirping songs. She wished she were a little bird and could fly away.

She set her jaw. If she let it, the guilt would swallow her whole like a boa swallowed a mouse. Then how would she help Nandan once she found him?

Sitting up, she wiped her cheeks and reached into her purse for the bottle of meds the doctor had prescribed for her. Back of the throat, easy swallow. She substituted the medicine bottle for her makeup bag.

A little repair work and she'd be as good as new.

She only hoped they'd believed her story about the heat.

6

"YES. THOSE SHOULD work great. Let's stop for the day."
Carly called to the crew, her voice echoing inside the
large cavern. "Thank you, everyone." She approached
Piper. "I realize the cave terrain was rough, but you
were fabulous."

Piper shrugged. "I'm just glad we're done. I need
a drink. Where's the nearest cantina?" She exited the
cave with a swish of her flowing sheer orange cover-
up. Her makeup and hair people followed in her wake
like courtiers of a queen.

And in her world she was royalty. Exquisitely beautiful. So photogenic. And Carly had to give her props.
Whatever had plagued her earlier, Piper had rallied.
After Joe had mentioned stress, Carly had started to
see Piper from a different perspective. Carly couldn't
imagine a life lived in the public eye 24/7. The months
following her father's arrest had been bad enough, between the hate mail and headlines, but at least she'd

been able to change schools and escape the scrutiny after a few weeks. Piper had no reprieve.

So, once Piper had reappeared from the taxi, Carly had offered to postpone the shoot for the day. But Piper had haughtily refused, and the pictures she'd taken were fabulous.

After the horrendous beginning, this day had ended by producing some amazing photos.

The few shots at the ruins were mainly about Joe and his transformation to modern-day pirate. He'd rocked the black jeans and billowing white shirt. And the boots?

One photo she knew would go into her personal album was of Joe standing on the bluff overlooking the sea, one booted foot raised on an outcropping of rock, his forearm resting on the raised knee. He was looking out to sea, his jaw covered in several days' growth of beard. The breezes ruffled his black hair and blew open the loose shirt. And there was just something about the look on his face. Women were going to swoon. Who was she trying to kid, she'd almost swooned.

After stopping at a local bar and grill for lunch, they'd directed the taxis to take them to Middle Caicos Island, and on the way, they drove past Flamingo Pond. Carly had never seen so many flamingos. The sight of so many bright pink birds flocked together in the blue water was breathtaking.

It seemed the only way to get to Middle Caicos, the least inhabited island, was driving across a rundown causeway. Carly dug her nails into her palms the whole way across. But the bridge held and they were soon at

Mudjin Harbor, a deserted beach so pristine that the shots they'd taken suggested Piper and Joe had been marooned on an island somewhere in the South Pacific.

That's when the distracting fantasy had begun. Of Joe and her, Carly, not Piper, alone together on an island paradise. No past. No future. No responsibilities. Only the here and now.

She pictured them feeding each other strawberries and lying in each other's arms on a towel on the beach…

And…she was doing it again.

What was wrong with her?

The final shots had been taken inside the largest cavern of Conch Bar Cave. Eerie and mysterious, the light and shadows had set just the right tone for the dramatic new summer collections *Modiste* wanted to feature.

Carly could hear Piper corralling most of the crew and convincing them to join her back on the ship at the nightclub. Car doors slammed as they piled into the taxis. Even Joe had followed Piper out.

And Carly was left alone. What was new? With her father's arrest, she'd become a pariah at seventeen. Girls she'd thought were her best friends had turned their backs on her. Her boyfriend had dropped her, and her prep school principal had gently suggested that her mother find a school "better suited to Carly's needs."

And nothing had changed since. She was still the daughter of Swindleton Pendleton. Ten years had passed, but the usual reaction to hearing her last name was, at best, distaste, at worst, overt hostility.

She raised her chin. So what? She didn't have time anyway. She had hours of work ahead of her.

Setting her jaw, she turned and bent to gather up her Gucci handbag, and her favorite Vera Wang wedge sandals she'd finally taken off due to the uneven terrain. She straightened to find Joe in her path.

He was standing so close her bag touched his arm. Though he had his cargo shorts and T-shirt gripped in one hand, he wore only the pair of lime green Abercrombie & Fitch swim shorts and brown leather flip-flops from the last pose. It meant his long, ridiculously muscled torso was left completely bare.

She resisted the urge to lift her hands and run them over his taut pecs. And she was doing okay feigning indifference until the breeze from the sea carried the scent of him crashing into her senses. She had to close her eyes and maybe she let a little moan escape, and with her eyes closed maybe she swayed just a bit, because he caught her upper arms and pulled her into him.

"What are you doing?" She met his gaze, irritation her only defense.

His eyes burned into hers. He didn't even bother to disguise what he wanted. He lowered his head but she averted her face.

"What's the matter?" He honestly sounded confused.

Carly heard taxis pulling away. "They're leaving."

"Yeah." He bent and pressed his lips to her neck. "I asked one of the drivers to come back for us in an hour."

His hot breath behind her ear made her shiver. "But." He trailed kisses up her neck. "We'll miss." More kisses and nibbles. "The plane."

"I cashed in a few favors and made arrangements with the pilot to come back for us." He captured her lips, wrapped an arm around her waist and cupped the back of her head with his other hand. Instinctively she dropped her bag and shoes and lifted her hands to his chest, sure that she meant to fight his hold, push him away. But, as his mouth plundered hers, she realized she was caressing him instead, from his collarbone to his ripped abs and back up to run her thumbs over his nipples.

He groaned into her mouth, tightened his hold. After last night she knew how sensitive his nipples were and reveled in his reaction. He angled his head to deepen the kiss, his lips moving over hers with a sense of desperation. Then abruptly he released her and scooped his clothes off the cave floor. "Come with me." His voice was rough and low. He took her hand and headed deeper into the cave.

Wait. Where was he going? She yanked her hand out of his and halted. "No. Call the taxi back."

His head whipped around, his expression incredulous. "Why?"

Let's see. How to put this?

She knew last night had been a huge mistake the minute he'd walked out of her room this morning. But rather than wallow in regret she'd told herself if he hadn't accidentally ended up in her cabin last night, it never would've happened. One night of incredible sex? Okay, she could deal. But more than that? Didn't that constitute an affair?

And affairs got messy.

Carly had tried a relationship once. She'd lived with Reese for almost a year. What a disaster that had turned into. Reese had started wanting more than just sex and splitting the rent. And Carly had discovered that she didn't have anything more to give.

One-night stands were more her thing. Satisfying. Fun. Uncomplicated.

Besides, even if she was able to make a man understand that she wanted nothing more than someone to escort her to the opera once or twice a year, Joe wasn't that guy. She had a feeling that, like Reese, he'd want more. Seeing the hurt in Reese's eyes had been bad enough. With Joe, the guilt would haunt her.

"I need to get back and work." She grabbed her shoes and bag.

He flashed that grin. "You'll have time to work later." He reached for her hand and tugged her, but she dug in her heels.

"I'm practically your employer. It's not ethical."

He raised his brows and gave her a skeptical look. "I promise I won't sue for harassment. Now, are you coming with me or should I throw you over my shoulder?"

She narrowed her eyes. "You wouldn't dare."

He grinned again. "You're right. I would never force anyone. But—" he stepped close and took her hand again "—I want to show you something I saw earlier during a break. Just come see this and then we'll go back."

She heard the words he'd left unspoken: *If you still want to.* Still, her curiosity was piqued. "All right."

JOE'S PULSE SPED UP as he touched the flashlight feature on his phone, shone it ahead of them and tugged Carly down the path that led farther into the cave system. Alone at last.

Maybe not the most romantic spot he'd ever taken a lady. The limestone columns that touched floor to ceiling were eerily alien at best, and stalagmites rising from the ground looked like people who'd been frozen into stone pillars. But the spot he'd found would make up for this part. And there was the adventure aspect of it all. He grinned, wondering how Carly would react to what he had in mind.

The path grew narrower, the ceiling lower, so he had to stoop to keep going. No way the camera and lighting equipment could've come through here safely.

"Joe, I don't like this. I'm not into surprises." Her hand gripped his like a lifeline.

"You don't need to be afraid. I wouldn't take you somewhere dangerous."

"I am *not* afraid."

If her icy tone could freeze humans, he'd be a cryogenics project right now. "Geez, okay. You're Ms. Fearless. Just a few more steps, around this corner…"

She gasped.

Bingo. He had her now. He stayed quiet, letting her take it all in. The beams of sunlight streaming in from the half dozen round holes carved through the cave wall sparkled on a little pond so perfect it could've been man-made. A waterfall splashed into the pond from a rock formation made of some iridescent stone that changed colors with every movement of water and sunlight.

"Oh, Joe." Her voice had gone all soft and breathy. "It's beautiful."

When he'd first gone exploring and found this place, he'd immediately pictured Carly in the water stripping down to only her bra and panties, floating in his arms and making love against the limestone. He'd been semi-erect the rest of the day thinking about this moment. "I asked the tour guide. It's safe to swim." Kicking off his sandals, he dimmed his cell phone's flashlight feature, set his clothes and cell down on a rock ledge and walked into the pond.

"Wait, what are you doing?"

Wading out to the deepest end, the water only came to his midchest. "Join me." He held out his hand.

She shook her head, crossed her arms over her chest, even took a step back. "I—I don't have a suit. And I'm not going to ruin these clothes."

He shrugged. "Take them off." He kept his hand extended, crooked his fingers in a sign for her to come to him. "It's okay. There won't be any more tours coming through tonight."

"No." She shook her head even more vigorously. If he didn't know better he'd say she was pouting.

"Come on, Carly. Where's the confident, take-no-prisoners woman I made love with last night? She was fearless and vibrant, up for any adventure." He squinted. "She's in there somewhere."

Her eyes flared in anger. "I'm the same person I always am."

He scoffed. What was going on with her? "Okay, I guess I've misread your signals. It's just that last night was…" He raised his hands out to his sides and let them fall back down. "Incomparable."

He waited, but she didn't say anything else. He wasn't going to break through her ice this time. He'd definitely been wrong about the connection he'd felt last night. "Well, at least you didn't deny the incomparable part."

With a sigh he strode out of the pond, grabbed his cell. "We can leave. I'll call a cab to come back for us."

"Wait." She covered his cell with her palm. Her hand was shaking. *She* was shaking.

Whoa. She really was uptight. "I just thought that if I'd told you ahead of time what I had in mind, I figured—"

"—that I'd turn you down."

"Yeah, there is that."

A rueful smile curved her beautiful lips. "If—If we do this, it can't interfere with the photo shoot. And what happens on the cruise ship, stays on the cruise ship. You can't let it affect—"

"Carly."

"What?"

With his arms around her, he bent her back and planted a big kiss on her mouth. "Take your clothes off already, will ya?"

Her response was in the form of sighs and moans as he kissed down her jaw and unbuttoned her shirt. She dropped her bag and shoes and unzipped the capris, wiggled them down her thighs and kicked them off.

Her arms tangled in her shirt sleeves as he tried to drag it off her and keep kissing her at the same time.

But finally she was down to her bra and panties and he lifted her up. She gave an approving little cry and wrapped her legs around his waist, cupping his face in her hands as she kissed him deep and deeper still.

Joe carried her into the pond, overwhelmed. Once she let go of her control, she lost her inhibitions. She ran her fingers through his hair and her sweet softness rubbed against his stiff length until he was silently begging for mercy. Hard to believe this was the same woman who'd been so reserved all day.

He set her down and stepped back to look at her, to slow down so things wouldn't be over before they began. She was breathing heavily, her pale skin flushed everywhere. Her panties and bra were a matching set of lavender lace. Her nipples peaked through the thin material. The silk panties turned transparent in the water.

She made a soft sound, a tiny moan and he raised his gaze to her face. Her long brunette hair fanned around her shoulders. He reached out to run his fingers through the strands curving around her face. "Do you have any idea how beautiful you look right now?"

She reached behind her with both hands and unhooked her bra, tossed it up on the path with her bag. Joe didn't bother holding back a strangled groan. Her breasts were like the rest of her: perfect. Round and full, with berry-colored nipples, beaded now into tight peaks. He had to touch them, feel her silky flesh, rub his thumbs over the tips.

She closed her eyes and let him play. He bent to lick, nibble, suckle. First one, then the other. With a whimper she cupped the back of his head. "Joe."

He loved hearing her say his name in that quivery voice. How she caught her breath on a gasp. How her frosty demeanor went out the window when she lost control.

As she bent to pull off her panties, Joe reached for his shorts on the ledge and grabbed the foil packet from the pocket.

He looked away, amazed that he was so close to the brink already. Flattening her hands on his chest she walked him back, deeper into the water. Her hands slid around his neck and she kissed his throat, her hands massaging his shoulders.

He groaned. "Carly?"

"Hmm?" She trailed kisses down his collarbone.

"You're killing me."

"I am?" She continued kissing his chest, then raised her gaze to his with a mischievous grin.

The smile undid him. Softened her face, changed her eyes from cold icy-blue to clear Caribbean-blue.

In one swift move, he cupped her bottom and waded across the water to set her on a smooth ledge. He hesitated, looked into her eyes. There was passion sparking in them, excitement, even delight. But as he held her gaze, it almost felt as if something more was happening between them. Emotion surged to the surface and he bent to place a soft kiss on her lips. She stilled, frowned, then lifted her calves around his hips to let him slide in.

Together they found a rhythm, moving as one.

With her head thrown back, he splayed a hand across her spine, the other kneading her soft breast. Nothing equaled the feeling of being inside a woman. It was pure, primal pleasure. And with the right woman? Ecstasy. She matched him thrust for thrust, making those sounds that told him she was close.

So was he. "Carly?"

"Yes." She leaned toward him and rested her forehead on his shoulder. "Now."

Joe thrust one last time, tensing as pleasure coursed through him, expanding from his stomach, to his chest, out to the ends of his fingertips. He couldn't breathe and shivered from the aftershock. He wrapped his arms around her waist, lifted her against him, and turned in the water. She clung to him, breathing heavily, her head tucked under his chin.

A sense of tenderness swept over him, filled him, made him want to keep this woman safe in his arms.

Whoa.

That didn't sound like a "what happens on the cruise stays on the cruise" kind of thought.

7

CARLY WOKE SLOWLY, her cheek pressed to hot, firm skin. She breathed in the scent of masculine sweat and the remains of whatever cologne she still hadn't identified. She opened her eyes. She was practically lying on top of Joe.

He was sleeping soundly. She carefully disentangled herself from his arms, climbed out of the warm bed and tiptoed to the restroom. Scrubbing a hand through her hair, she gripped the edges of the sink and studied her reflection in the mirror.

The face looking back at her was barely recognizable. Were those *her* lips, so swollen from kissing? She turned her head and lifted her chin. Her cheeks and neck were chafed from Joe's rough stubble. Her hair was a rat's nest, and her eyes were puffy.

What were you thinking, girl?

She hadn't thought.

Her brain had taken a vacation. And it had been marvelous. The shipboard fantasy had been a much needed break from the hectic schedule she'd been keeping.

Carly couldn't remember the last time she'd taken even a weekend off. Not since college. Maybe not even then....

After her father's scandal, her mother had pretty much been MIA. In less than a month Carly had changed to a public school, taken a job in the exciting field of fast food and started looking at state universities. Even then it'd taken her six years to earn her degree while she worked full-time.

The past couple of days had been like...like playing hooky. A guilty pleasure. For just a short while she'd allowed herself to be carefree. To fantasize that she could have a real relationship with a guy. Every morning since the caves at Caicos Island, she'd told herself this had to stop. They couldn't continue to sneak away after each photo shoot and spend the rest of the night making love like a couple of insatiable teens. She'd tell herself she had photos to look over, to decide which ones she'd submit to *Modiste* for the magazine spread, and which ones she'd use in her blog. This was her one chance to make the big leagues. The opportunity she'd been working so hard for.

And then the day's photo shoot would end, and Joe would somehow manage to talk her into going off with him. They'd ridden horses down the beach at Half Moon Cay, and then made love in a deserted cove. And after getting some fabulous shots in The Retreat National Park in Nassau, with its lush palms and exotic flowers, Joe had whisked her off to more unoccupied parts of the eleven-acre woodland. They'd made love inside a dilapidated arbor hidden among the flourishing overgrown foliage.

Both nights, once they'd made it back to the ship, they'd spent the rest of the evening in her cabin wrapped in each other's arms. It wasn't like her to act so impulsively. But then, Joe wasn't like any guy she'd ever met. He tempted her. He distracted her from her goals.

Stepping into the shower, she let the hot water spray her face. She had to get Joe out of her head and get her life back on track. None of this made any sense.

She'd just shampooed her hair when the door opened and Joe stepped in behind her. "Morning," he mumbled at her neck as he slid his arms around to cup her breasts. The heat from his body enveloped her. His scent melted her resistance. Everything about him rendered her weak.

"I was thinking, once we get back, we could—"

"Please, Joe. I can't."

He stilled. An awkward moment hung heavily in the air until he dropped his arms. "I get it." She felt him shrug. "Cruise is over, right?" Then he stepped out.

Carly stood under the steaming water, motionless as Joe dried with a towel and left the small bathroom. She clenched her teeth. Why should she feel guilty? He'd known the score from the beginning.

With a sigh, she shut off the water and grabbed a towel. When she padded into the main cabin, Joe was dressed and sitting on the bed putting on his shoes.

"Look, Joe, I—"

"I said I get it. No explanation necessary." He stood,

went over to the dressing counter and shoved his wallet and key card into his pocket.

Carly tucked the towel tighter around herself, her wet hair dripping down her back. "It's just that I barely have time for sleep right now. All my energy is focused on making a success of my blog. I was in a relationship a couple of years ago. The guy got tired of barely seeing me. He wanted more and I didn't blame him. But I wasn't willing to give up my dream." She paused. "I'm still not."

Joe moved to her side. He cupped her cheek with his palm, bent and gave her a soft kiss on the mouth. "Thanks for the honesty."

She bit her lip. What else was there to say?

He nodded, then left the cabin, shutting the door behind him.

He was gone. She closed her eyes, rubbed her stomach where it burned. Did she have indigestion? And there was a lump in her throat.

It didn't matter. Real life wasn't a cruise ship vacation. Real life was about achieving her goals. It was about making something of herself that had nothing to do with being the daughter of Charles Pendleton.

She couldn't afford to slow down her pace, to let herself go soft. Joe was a great guy. But he'd never survive a relationship with her. Reese hadn't. And there was no sense putting herself—or Joe—through that kind of heartache.

Still, she wished he was here. Missed his big warm body and strong arms around her.

And his smile.

And that way he had of making her feel as though everything was going to be okay. That *she* was okay.

What was she thinking? Of course she was okay. Irritated, she quickly dressed and applied her makeup. She packed and set her luggage in the hallway for the steward and went to the upper deck.

The next hour was chaotic directing everyone involved with the shoot off the ship and through customs in the Miami terminal and then making sure everyone got rides to the airport with their boarding passes for New York.

As usual there was a commotion around Piper. The model was complaining about waiting in line, people crammed around her, snapping pictures with their cell phones. Carly approached her to let her know the limo was waiting with her favorite brand of champagne and chocolate-covered strawberries when she heard a high-pitched yapping echo from the exit.

Piper cried out and darted out of line. "Pootsie!" She raced past the customs officers, her arms outstretched.

Carly followed Piper's trajectory past customs to see the supermodel's short assistant carrying the yelping dog in her arms. Then, Carly watched in horror as all proverbial hell broke loose.

The dog escaped the assistant's arms, jumped to the floor and scrambled toward Piper.

Customs officers chased Piper, grabbed her arms and tried to drag her back to the check-in area.

Piper shrieked and began fighting the officers like a wild animal would fight capture. "Do you know who I am? How dare you? Take your hands off me!" As phones videoed and cameras flashed, she stomped her stiletto heel onto one officer's boot and slammed her enormous bag into the other's head, knocking him down.

Two more officers ran to help.

Carly stood helplessly as Piper was subdued and handcuffed.

Of course, the crowd was in a frenzy of gleeful cellphone videography.

Piper was screaming. Her assistant already had a phone to her ear, calling, Carly presumed, Piper's agent. Better still, her lawyer.

Piper wrenched out of the guard's hold and swiveled to scream at Carly. "This is *your* fault."

And suddenly the officers were scrutinizing her.

"I'm only on this cruise because of her. Do you know who she is?" Piper continued, loud enough for everyone in the vicinity to hear. "That's Charles Pendleton's daughter. She's got all that money her father stole. You should be arresting her!"

Carly looked around the terminal. Travelers had gathered to gawk. Just like before. People staring at her. Wondering how she was involved. Judging her.

One of the guards dropped Piper's arm and approached her. "Ma'am, is this woman with your party?"

Carly's stomach cramped and nausea rose until she tasted bile. "Yes."

"Would you come with us, please?" the officer asked.

The gray walls of the terminal wobbled out of focus. Memories hit her with a sickening thud. Having to sit in court while her father glared at the jury. Reporters swarming wherever she went. Asking her if she'd known of her dad's crimes. The people who had spit at her, called her horrible names. And her so-called friends? She'd had to change schools after she was dragged into a bathroom and harassed by a group of classmates whose parents her father had swindled out of millions.

As she swayed she felt callused hands catch her elbows and gently guide her to a chair.

"Put your head between your legs. Take a deep breath." It was Joe's voice, soothing, calm.

She tried to speak but it seemed her jaw was locked. Her teeth chattered.

Because it was happening all over again. She'd be questioned by the police. Scrutinized by the media. The magazine would blame her. She was responsible for this photo shoot. Once the scandal was linked with *Modiste,* Carly's career would be over. Four years of coming home from the sixty-hour-a-week day job to add new content to her interactive blog, of interning for designers, building relationships with department-store buyers. Every new reader a triumph, every new ad on her blog a sign that she might just make it.

Now her dreams were disintegrating into ashes.

"Carly!" Gentle fingers threaded through her hair and lifted her face. "Baby, look at me."

Carly blinked and Joe's dark brown eyes came into focus.

"Breathe."

She did as he asked. Such beautiful brown eyes. Kind eyes.

"That's it. Now let it out slowly."

She released her breath. He had such kissable lips. The bottom lip was fuller than the top. Soft, yet masculine. The things those lips had done to her.

"That's good." He turned his attention to someone outside their little world. "Where's that bottle of water?"

"Here. Take a sip of water." He held a bottle to her lips.

Joe. So sweet. Caring for her. Carly longed to lean into him, have him wrap his arms around her and make all her troubles go away.

And that's exactly why she wouldn't. She wasn't some weak waif who needed rescuing. Joe had worn that same worried expression when Piper'd had her panic attack.

Carly touched his cheek. "Thank you, I'm all right now. Cristoph!" She got to her feet, calling to the makeup artist, motioning for him to come close. He'd been a friend since they'd worked at the same Manhattan salon and spa back in college. She knew she could count on him. "I've got to see what I can do to help Piper. Can you make sure the store liaisons get their clothes safely onto the flight to New York, please?"

Cristoph nodded, and immediately began directing the clothing handlers, the hair and makeup teams, and the *Modiste* liaison to the exit.

One worry over, she headed for the customs search area. Maybe she could still save Piper. Talk to her attorney, maybe avoid any charges before they were ever officially made. If this mess concerning Piper didn't go away fast, Carly could kiss her contract with *Modiste* Magazine goodbye.

Hadn't *Modiste* realized the young supermodel was a walking terror? The girl's photo was splashed all over the front covers of the tabloids for hard partying and losing her temper with the paparazzi. But she was the hottest model out there and Carly had gone with the decision figuring a successful shoot would outweigh any problems.

Carly sighed. Piper was her responsibility for now. And all she could hope for was containment.

The customs officer was waiting for her to accompany him and, clenching her fists, she strode with him and Piper's assistant to the room where Piper was being detained.

When she glanced back, Joe was nowhere to be seen.

SHE NEEDED HER PILLS.

It took Piper three tries to cover her face with her scarf, her hands were shaking so badly. Of course the handcuffs didn't help. She lowered her chin as she stepped out of the cruise terminal, prepared to be bombarded by the paparazzi. She could've told Carly that waiting until all the other passengers had left wouldn't make a difference. The parasites who made their living off the lives of others wouldn't be deterred.

"Piper! Over here!" One pest called to her above the din of shouting cameramen.

Cameras flashed like fireworks popping all around her and she tucked her face into her arm, letting the officers lead her down the gangway to the waiting police car.

Shame filled her as she sat in the back and lowered her head to her knees. She'd never committed a crime before. Well, not since she'd been a starving child. Why did she do these things? She didn't understand her reckless behavior. But sometimes she felt as if she would burst inside if she didn't scream at the world. And when that feeling took over, she didn't care about consequences, or who got hurt. Even herself.

What would happen to her now? Her career was at its peak. And she had gone through so much to get to this point. She had fame, financial stability and could go anywhere, live anywhere she wanted to. But in this moment what she really wanted was to be left alone. No, that wasn't right, either. What she really wanted was to be with her brother.

Could she just pay a fine and maybe perform some community service? In the customs detainee room, Carly had suggested she ask her agent to retain a good defense attorney.

She closed her eyes and prayed. If only she could get out of this with a light sentence she'd…

She had no incense, no garlands or vermilion, and if she'd ever been taught the songs of praise, she didn't remember them now. The gods would not listen to her.

But people bargained with their gods, didn't they? What hated thing could they require of her?

The answer came to her in a whispered voice.

If she received a light sentence and was not sent to prison, she would go back to rehab. And vow to be good from now on.

8

AH, IT WAS good to be home in New York! This city was full of people just like Carly. Focused. Ambitious. Impatient.

She stood at the circular baggage claim at JFK tapping her foot. Checking her cell. Waiting for her luggage.

The Piper fiasco had gone badly and an assistant editor from *Modiste* had texted that they wanted a meeting tomorrow, but at least she had today to recover and prepare.

They couldn't blame her for what had happened, could they? Would they decide not to publish her photos in their magazine now? Until she knew something more, she could only proceed as normal.

Pulling up the contacts on her cell, she texted Piper's manager, then the legal department at *Modiste* to follow up on Piper's arrest. She daydreamed of pouring herself a glass of Chardonnay and soaking in a tub until her skin turned all wrinkled. But that wasn't going to happen. Thanks to her cruise-ship fling she was way behind on sorting through the photos on her laptop. She had to decide which ones to submit. Narrowing them down wouldn't be easy. Piper and Joe had taken some phenomenal shots. But there were a couple of solos of Joe...

She couldn't believe she'd let herself get involved with her contest winner. What had she been thinking?

Joe appeared at the other side of the baggage carousel and hadn't spotted her yet.

"Joey!" A short, plump woman with salt-and-pepper hair rushed to *Joey* with her arms outstretched. Joe wrapped his arms around the lady and hugged her with an expression of such love...Carly's chest ached.

Before she could dig an antacid from her purse the guy was surrounded by a mob of dark-haired people who all resembled each other and him. She'd never seen so many large white-teethed smiles. Everyone had to hug him and kiss his cheek and hang on to him. A short gray-haired lady even pinched his cheek.

There had to be at least half a dozen of them clinging to his arms and talking all at once. It made Carly claustrophobic on his behalf. But he didn't seem to mind. He smiled and returned hugs and stooped to pick up a hyper toddler while keeping one muscled arm around his mother. The woman was patting his cheek and gesturing with her hands as she talked. Good grief. The way they all acted you'd think he'd been missing for years instead of on vacation for five days.

And yet, as Carly watched them all standing around talking with each other, they seemed more than just happy to see Joe. These people were a unit. A cohesive group. They seemed bonded to each other by more than just bloodlines. They seemed…to truly love each other.

Yeah. Probably last two minutes. Once they got in the car they'd be at each other's throats. That's what families did.

She was about to check her vibrating cell when Joe looked over at her. His smile slowly disappeared.

Carly stepped away from the carousel and raised the phone to her ear, pretending to talk. Hoping that would deter him.

After a couple of minutes of fake phone conversation she ventured a peek in his direction. He was headed for the exit, arm in arm with the older woman who was probably his mother, with kids hanging on to his legs and arms, jumping around him. Her throat tightened. *What a sap.*

But did she mean Joe? Or herself?

Where had that thought come from? Shaking her head in self-disgust, she spied her suitcase on the carousel and moved to grab it. Once outside, she hailed a taxi and spent the ride texting with Piper's manager. He tried to convince Carly they could spin the arrest disaster into a win for the magazine. *Modiste* would only sell *more* copies because of the scandal. He agreed to meet her at *Modiste's* offices tomorrow morning and maybe together they could convince the editor.

That settled for the moment, she dragged her luggage up the three flights to her studio apartment, kicked off her heels and padded over to the refrigerator.

Maybe she'd have that glass of Chardonnay after all.

"BUT, JOEY, I made sausage meatballs."

Joe smiled indulgently at his mother. She knew he couldn't resist the house specialty. "Okay, Ma. I'll stay."

After the wait getting through customs, the second rejection from Carly in the cruise terminal and the long flight to JFK, he just wanted to go home to his own place and pop open a beer in front of the TV.

He needed time to sort out all the crazy things he was thinking and feeling. But that would have to wait. All four of his older siblings, their spouses and their kids just happened to be hanging at Ma and Pop's. And it wasn't even Sunday. You'd think no one in their family had ever been on a cruise before.

"Geez, Al, isn't this a school night?" Joe asked as two of his nephews started fighting over the PlayStation.

"Are you kiddin'? I want to hear all about the supermodel. What's her name? Paulina?"

Alfonso's wife hitched their toddler higher on her hip and rolled her eyes.

"It's Piper," his other brother, Bernardo, contributed. "What was she like, Joey? Sexy, I'll bet."

Joe cleared his throat and headed toward the group of kids in front of the TV. "How many of you rug rats want your presents now?" He opened his duffel and pulled out the cruise-ship gift-shop bag full of toys and stuffed animals.

All the kids except Rosalie's newborn jumped and squealed as he distributed the souvenirs.

"Joey, you shouldn't have," Donna-Marie exclaimed, shoving his shoulder when he handed her a miniature sailor's uniform for baby Alberto.

Joe shrugged and settled at the big kitchen table as his loud family gathered around, all talking at once. His ma snuck him a plate of meatballs with a wink. His dad lounged in his recliner and tried to pretend he was reading the paper while kids crawled all over him. His parents' house was like Brooklyn itself. It never changed. It just got more crowded and noisier. Which was great most of the time.

But he kept picturing Carly standing all alone at the airport. Her lips pinched, her brow creased. He'd wanted to go to her, put his arm around her and assure her the thing with Piper would blow over. But she'd made it clear she didn't want or need his comfort. He had to accept that and move on. What they'd had was just a vacation thing.

"So, did you take lots of pictures?" Rosalie snatched his cell phone from his shirt pocket.

"Hey!" He tried to grab it back but she tossed it over to Donna-Marie.

Joe folded his arms. He wasn't "Little Joey" anymore, and he refused to play keep-away. Sometimes being the baby of the family still sucked. Even if he was a foot taller than either of his sisters.

Donna-Marie clicked his phone open to his photos. "Oooh, is this the pool on the ship?"

"I want to see." Rosie raced over to her sister and leaned in to stare at the phone screen.

"Meet any nice girls there?" Donna-Marie swiped to the next photo. "Who's this?" She turned the phone so the entire room could see a picture of Carly on the ship. As with most of the pictures he had of her, he'd taken it when she wasn't looking.

"Whoa." His brother-in-law Gino stilled from filling his mouth with meatballs. "You hit that hottie?"

"None of your business." Joe made a grab for his phone, but his sister twisted away and swiped his phone several more times. Gino eyed him smugly.

Rosie giggled. "Geez, Joey, you got enough pictures of her in here. Come on, is she your new girlfriend?"

Joe clenched his teeth and glanced heavenward. "She's not my girlfriend. She was just the director of the photo shoot."

"You have a girlfriend, Joey?" His mother stopped stirring her sauce and turned from the stove.

Great. Now they'd done it. "No, Ma."

"Then how come you have so many pictures of her?" Rosie asked.

His ma's eyes widened and gleamed with hope. "Is she a nice girl, Joey?"

He was going to kill his sister. Slowly. For almost a decade now Ma had been obsessed with him finding a nice girl, settling down and giving her grandkids. She already had twelve but that apparently was not enough progeny. "Ma. She's not my girlfriend. Carly is just the blogger who ran the contest."

"This is *the* Carly, from *Carly's Couture?*" Rosie asked.

"Ooh, we love her blog!" Donna-Marie added.

"You bring her to dinner Sunday, Joey," Ma ordered. "I want to meet this girl you took so many pictures of."

She punctuated her command by poking her wooden spoon in his direction.

"Yeah, Joe, bring her to dinner Sunday." His older sister smirked.

Joe closed his eyes. Counted to ten. Then he lunged at his sister, seized his phone and shoved it into his duffel bag. "I'm heading home."

"Oh, we restocked your fridge and watered your plants, baby brother," Donna-Marie called as he strode toward the front door. "And you had a lot of mail at the firehouse and your chief asked us to come get it, so we left it on your table."

"Mail? At the firehouse?" Joe stopped halfway to the door.

Rosie giggled.

"Fan mail." Donna-Marie smiled knowingly. "From women who saw that you won Carly's contest."

Joe groaned. Shook his head. He was going to kill his sisters.

BEAUTY BEHIND BARS!
Supermodel Piper Arrested for Drug Smuggling
Shocking Link to Swindleton Scandal

Carly pitched the worst of the tabloids across her kitchen table and knocked back the last of her coffee in one swallow. A glance at her coffeemaker showed the carafe was empty. It didn't matter. There wasn't enough caffeine in the world to make the emptiness in her gut go away.

Facing the editor yesterday had taken every ounce

of her nerve. Just getting to the meeting at *Modiste* had been agony. The minute she'd stepped outside to catch a cab dozens of microphones had been stuck in her face. Cameras rolled while reporters yelled at her for a comment. Or worse; shouted questions about her father.

When she arrived at the *Modiste* offices in Times Square, she'd been shown into a conference room by an intern and had waited almost thirty minutes before Ms. Cauzan, the managing editor, and her team showed up. Piper's manager walked in beside the senior editor all buddy-buddy. Carly had taken that as a sign that things weren't going to go well for her.

After making sure Carly had been offered a beverage, Ms. Cauzan had recommended they get right to the business at hand. She'd taken her seat at the head of the long table and folded her hands on its gleaming surface. "Piper's attorney has accepted a plea bargain on her behalf. She'll get probation and ninety days community service."

Piper's manager had nodded and smiled at the editor, studiously avoiding eye contact with Carly.

Ms. Cauzan had cleared her throat. She gave the man seated on her left—probably an attorney—a meaningful look, and then brought her cold gaze back to Carly. "The photos of Piper and your contest winner will be published in the May publication as agreed. But, unfortunately, we've decided not to bring your blog in-house. *Modiste* will be taking their online presence in a different direction." With that, she'd stood, indicating the meeting was over. Her team got to their feet, as well.

So, Piper's manager had been right. The powers at

Modiste believed Piper's titillating—and temporary—fall from grace would ultimately sell more magazines. But Carly's connection to a billion-dollar Ponzi scheme was not the right kind of publicity.

Carly had suspected they would do this, yet the news still hit her with a hard thud. Somehow she'd managed to nod and smile, keep her expression pleasant and shake everyone's hands.

Of course *Modiste* had known of her connection to Swindleton Pendleton when they offered to sponsor the contest on her blog. However, at that time her father's scandal was old news. It had happened ten years ago. The world had moved on. Now, though, public outrage over her father's criminal activities had been brought to the forefront once again. And *Modiste* wouldn't want any association with him.

Carly didn't remember much of the cab ride back to her apartment. She'd been pleasantly numb until the taxi pulled in front of her building and she'd had to run the gauntlet of greedy paparazzi.

Twenty-four hours later and the memory still stung.

Her cell rang, and the tone startled her. She fumbled as she grabbed it to check the ID. And suppressed a groan. Not now. The ringtone taunted her while she debated answering. If she didn't talk to her mother now, Vicky would keep phoning until she did. Resigned, she touched Accept. "Hello, Mother."

"Carly, how could you do this to me?" Her mother's wail held just the perfect amount of wobbly voiced sobbing punctuated by sniffles.

Carly gritted her teeth. "It will blow over soo—"

"How can you be so calm? Do you know what I've had to go through today? I had to cancel my spa appointment and my trainer won't brave the vultures gathered outside my house. And now I've got a migraine coming on, I can just feel it."

Spas and trainers? Carly knew her mother's new husband had a lucrative cosmetic-surgery practice in Taos, but still.… There was always that niggling traitorous question in the deep recesses of Carly's mind. Had her mother known about her father's illegal scheme? "Mother, you need to calm down."

"That's easy for you to say, but I can't leave my house. I can't go to lunch. I can't meet my friends. They certainly can't come over here, Carly. It's happening all over again. This is just like after your father…"

Carly tuned out the rest of her mother's rant. She knew exactly what it had been like. Her mother had fallen apart and Carly had been left to pick up the pieces.

For the first few months after her father's arrest, Carly had been haunted by his crimes. Every major newspaper, magazine and television newscast had skewered Charles Pendleton. And deservedly so. But the media had decided she and her mother were guilty by association. Even though she'd been completely clueless about her father's actions.

At school, she'd heard whispered slurs. Crooked Carly or Carly Swindleton. Every friend had deserted her. She'd been ostracized, and, if she was lucky, ignored. She'd been forced to change to a public school her senior year, where at least most of her classmates weren't from families her father had defrauded.

Then, while she was in college, he went to trial and it had started all over again.

It'd taken her years to pull together some semblance of a normal life. By the time she'd earned her degree she'd vowed that someday she'd redefine the name Pendleton.

"Carly? Are you even listening?"

Carly blinked. "Yes, Mother."

"If you had just changed your last name this wouldn't be happening."

"Which stepfather's name should I have taken, Mother?" Somehow, changing her name had seemed like denying who she really was. And, maybe a part of her had just wanted to defy her mother.

"Well at least I have a man. You can't even manage to keep a boyfriend, much less a husband."

"I support myself, Mother."

"Support? You've struggled with that blog for years and where has it gotten you?"

"Uh, thirty thousand followers and recognition from *Modiste* magazine!"

"Really? That many? And *Modiste* magazine?" There was a speculative tone in her voice. "Are they going to buy you out? Carly, you could make millions. Oh, that's Simon on the other line. Talk later." The line went dead.

Wow. Good thing she had no illusions about her mother. The relationship was what it was.

At the time of the scandal Carly had made the excuse

that Vicky was too distraught to see how miserable her daughter was. Her mother had hated losing the house and her status. They'd moved into a budget motel, and, for a while, the district attorney had even investigated Vicky as a possible accessory to her husband's pyramid scheme. But within six months Vicky had remarried and moved to Florida, leaving Carly alone. Carly had scrambled to find a place to live and taken a second job.

Other than a few phone calls, she hadn't heard from her mother again until Vicky showed up on her doorstep with the news that her marriage was over. She'd stayed with Carly a couple of weeks—Carly slept on the sofa—until Vicky met and ran off with her current husband. And that was the beginning of seeing her mother only when she got bored with Taos and needed a New York fix.

At least she'd checked into a hotel the past couple of times. And Carly's second job had been serendipitous. Sewing at night for an apparel manufacturer in the garment district had given her a look at the world of fashion from the inside out.

Carly returned to the kitchen table, sat and opened her laptop. The photos from the cruise still needed to be sorted and the ones to be used for the magazine spread chosen. She opened the folder, determined to— Oh, that one of Joe was… She bit her lip.

Sexy. Joe was sitting on the outcropping of rocks on the beach, his elbow on his raised knee, and that smile. He seemed to be looking directly through the camera at Carly. And the smolder in his eyes. How could any woman resist a man who was so steamingly sensual? Steamingly? Was that even a word?

Who cared?

She didn't want to stop reliving their nights together, the way he'd made love to her. She imagined his tanned skin radiating heat, defining muscle. His hands touching her, pleasuring her. His large body moving over her, entering her...

She closed her eyes, remembering the feel of his lips devouring hers, his tongue—oh, the things he'd done with his tongue. Something wet dropped onto her forearm and she blinked. Crying? She never cried. She was just stressed. She blotted a tissue under her eyes, careful not to smudge her mascara. There'd been all the work on the contest, then the travel and directing the photo shoot, and then yesterday she'd had to worry about putting out fires at *Modiste*.

Putting out fires? Oh, no. What had made her come up with that metaphor? Did everything have to remind her of Joe?

Joe... She studied the photo of him again. What was he doing right now? Was he at work? Sitting around the firehouse? Or was he off work? Home? Maybe on a date or...had he brought his date back to his place for the night? A deluge of images flooded her brain. Of him naked, sprawled on a bed with some beautiful woman.

Stop!

She'd never pined over some guy. And she wasn't going to start now. It'd been a fun fling. Great sex. But it was over. And she had work to do.

Straightening her spine, she grabbed her cell phone.

Screw the paparazzi camped in front of her apartment building. She ordered her usual dim sum for one and then went to run a bath.

She would look at the photos later tonight. After a meal, and her scented bath oils, and some Pilates restored her equilibrium. After she'd steeled her mind to see Joe Tedesco as just a model in a photo shoot.

She would do this.

"ANJU RAJARAMAN, how do you plead?"

Piper startled at the sound of her real name coming from the judge's lips.

"She pleads no contest, Your Honor." Her attorney spoke for her. He'd advised her to not admit guilt but to take the plea bargain of no contest in exchange for a lowered charge of assault—only a misdemeanor—as opposed to aggravated assault, which carried a mandatory term in a penitentiary.

"Very well, the fine is set at five thousand dollars and time served." The judge banged his gavel and that was it. She was free to go.

"Thank you." Piper shook the lawyer's hand, then turned to Ragi, her dear friend standing behind her, the only one who really knew her and understood. "Let's go home." Piper slipped her arm through hers.

They'd stayed at The Palms awaiting her court date. The Miami resort hotel was accustomed to catering to celebrities' needs and it was as good a place as any to try to hide from the press and the paparazzi.

"No." Ragi pulled her arm from Piper's.

"What do you mean no?" Piper saw the deep sadness

in Ragi's eyes and frowned. "We can't hang out here any longer. I've got work in New York."

"Then you must return there without me. New York is destroying you. You must find peace, Anju."

Piper glanced around the courtroom, and then leaned in to whisper. "We'll talk somewhere else, okay?"

"What difference does it make now? How could anyone think any worse of you than they already do?"

Piper looked closer at Ragi. Her face was sallow. There were dark circles under her eyes. "You aren't well?" She spoke to her in their native language of Hindi but Ragi replied in English.

"I'm fine. It is you who is sick." She placed her palm over her upper chest. "In here."

Piper had no answer for that. She shrugged. "There's nothing I can do about that."

"There is. Be honest with the therapists at the rehab center you go to. Tell them how lonely you are, even when you're in a crowd or with a group of friends. Tell them about how you miss your brother. How you can't sleep at night."

Piper stiffened even before Ragi finished speaking. "Please." She scoffed. "What can that help? They probably wouldn't understand anyway. People who don't really know what loss is, can't talk about it or advise—"

"Joe recommended this lady. She's helped a friend of his whose wife died when their towers were struck."

"Joe? How would he know someone in Florida?"

"His friend was a college roommate who grew up here and he moved back after his wife died so his children could be near his parents and his wife's parents."

"Ragi, please. I just want to get back to work."

Her friend frowned. She looked skeptical. "I'll always be grateful to you for the opportunity you gave me. But I can't watch you destroy yourself." Her friend bent to reach for her handbag and slung it over her shoulder, then straightened to face her, her chin raised stubbornly. "You must find a new assistant.."

Piper couldn't believe this was happening. "But what will I do without you?"

The sadness in Ragi's eyes darkened and they welled with tears. "I don't know." She wrapped an arm around her shoulder. "Goodbye, Anju."

Piper returned her hug with both arms and didn't let go even when Ragi tried to pull away.

9

"WELL, LOOK WHO showed up. Mr. Sexy!" Wakowski struck a pose with one hand behind his head and the other on his hip as Joe entered the fire-station rec room. With his barrel chest and bald head, Wakowski looked more like a trucker having a seizure.

"Hey, Joe! You gonna be America's next hot model?"

"Well, if it ain't little Joey back from paradise!"

The other guys greeted Joe as they stood from where they'd been sitting in front of the TV.

Joe lifted his hands and crooked his fingers. "Come on. Get it over with."

Everman smirked. "We gonna see you modeling underwear on the jumbotron in Times Square now?"

Stockton snickered. "He's probably gonna pose for the fireman's calendar."

Joe smiled and nodded while the guys hooted and catcalled. "You guys are just jealous." He tossed his duffel onto a cot, then strode to the foosball table and grabbed the 5-bar and the 3-bar rods.

"Course we are, Tedesco." Wakowski answered as the guys followed him, gathering around the game table.

"So, Joe. You and Piper, eh?" Miller waggled his brows and elbowed him in the ribs.

"You losers gonna play or what?" Joe spun the 3-bar rod, hitting the ball toward the goal.

"Seriously." Wakowski grabbed the goalie rod and blocked the ball, hitting it back into play. "Did you know the contest lady was Swindleton's daughter? What was she like?"

Joe shoved his 3-bar forward and spun, trying for the goal again and missed. "How'd you guys know about that?"

"It's everywhere, dude." Miller grabbed the 2-bar rod, playing defense.

"Yeah, who *doesn't* know about it?" Wakowski said, jostling a rod back and forth, blocking another potential goal.

Stockton nodded. "Try the *Daily Scoop*." He tossed a tabloid at Joe's chest, and then joined the game, gripping a steel rod.

The game forgotten, Joe caught the newspaper, glanced at the front page, and there was Carly's picture in a full-color eight by ten. Why did the gossip rags have to choose the most unflattering images? The photographer had caught her glowering at someone off camera. The headline insinuated that she was spending her daddy's ill-gotten millions on luxurious beach vacations. Ouch.

That had to hurt. He knew how hard she'd worked during the cruise. How she'd bristled when he'd asked her about her connection to Pendleton at their initial meeting. She'd tried to hide her reaction, as if she didn't care who knew or remembered, but he'd noticed her shoulders had stiffened and her chin had raised just a notch. And that defensive glitter in her eyes. Oh, he'd gotten to know that look pretty well.

And he missed it.

He flung the tabloid at the garbage and took up the game again. "Pizza's on me tonight, boys."

The guys cheered and set to playing foosball with gusto, and, for now at least, the subjects of Carly and modeling in his underwear were dropped.

But before they could phone in their usual pizza order, the alarm rang and they raced to their boots and coats, sliding down the pole and jumping on the engine as it pulled out of the garage. An apartment fire. They were never good. It took all night to extinguish the spreading fire and make sure everyone was evacuated, including a cantankerous cat. But a little kid was wailing about finding his kitty.

Joe's oxygen tank was almost empty as he and Miller went in after the pet. The heat was so intense, Joe thought they might have to leave it. The whole floor was about to go. Deciding he'd give it a couple of more minutes, he signaled to Miller to wait in the hall. Miller gestured the affirmative and advised the chief of their location.

Joe crawled through the front room to another door, felt for heat behind it, then opened it and went through. The smoke blinded him and he couldn't hear any meows in the apartment for the roar of the fire. Their chief came over the walkie-talkie ordering them to get out. Joe relayed a request for five more minutes, then turned down the volume, stilled and closed his eyes. *Come on, Kitty. Help me help you.* He held his breath and tuned his hearing to the sounds beneath the sounds. And waited.

Then he heard it. The faintest hint of a high-pitched meow. Crouching low, he followed the sound, ducking under a collapsing door frame, dodging falling debris until he caught sight of the cat. He turned up the volume on his walkie-talkie, reported his position, then grabbed the cat by the scruff of its neck and hightailed it toward the exit, following Miller to the stairwell. They'd barely reached it as exploding fire enveloped the floor.

The blast propelled Joe down the stairs. He landed hard on his side, his temple slammed against a brick wall. For a moment the room spun. Where was Miller? He looked up and the ceiling above him was buckling. This might be it. Any minute he could be buried beneath the rubble. His mother would kill him if he died. Okay, that was stupid. Then, even more stupidly, he thought of Carly. He wanted more time with her.

Suddenly hands were dragging him to his feet and Stockton and Everman helped him down to the bottom of the stairs. Miller took the cat and just as Joe's vision cleared, he saw Wakowski handing it to the crying kid.

A paramedic ran up and began administering first aid to Joe, examining his sore shoulder and bleeding temple. And the chief stalked over to yell at him about taking unnecessary risks. But this was why he loved what he did. "Look at that kid's face, Chief. You wouldn't want to be the one to tell him Mr. Whiskers didn't make it, would you?"

"I don't want to have to tell your mother her little Joey didn't make it!" the chief yelled, his face red, a vein in his temple bulging.

"Chief, I told him to go," Miller tried.

But the chief only snarled. "Either one of you do that again, you're suspended, you got me?"

Joe nodded. His chief was right. That had been too close. He shouldn't have risked it. He'd had a couple of minutes to think about his death in there. It's not as though he was a thrill-seeker, but it was a given that he had a dangerous job. All his friends and family knew that. Still, he guessed it was one thing to acknowledge a loved one had a dangerous job, and another to have to face his death.

He knew his family would grieve. His mother, especially. But at least he wouldn't leave a widow, or make kids fatherless. Miller, heck, all the other guys had wives, kids. He didn't know how the rest of his ladder coped with that.

He supposed with the right kind of woman, a strong, independent woman who had her own life and wasn't totally dependent on him…he wouldn't have to worry so much.

What a thought that was.

When he got home to his empty apartment after his twenty-four-hour shift, he had to dodge a sneaky cameraman hiding down the stairs to the basement. He thought of Carly again. How was she handling the brutal media storm?

The headlines were all about Piper's return to New York and her conspicuous absence from the nightclub scene. The front-page photo was of Piper, but the story still mentioned Carly and her connection to her father. It insinuated that she lived off the money he'd cheated from honest hardworking people.

Joe had spent five days with her. Well, four. And three nights in her bed. In every imaginable position. And some he hadn't imagined. Great. Now his jeans were uncomfortable. Grabbing a beer from the fridge, he held the cold bottle to his forehead.

Despite the great sex, he knew next to nothing about her. Maybe he should just give her a call. Make sure she was weathering the media attention okay. He could follow up on the release date for the magazine. Had she said his picture would be in the May issue? Or the June? Either way, he wanted some kind of warning so he could prepare for when his family went berserk.

Yeah. That's all he wanted. Information on the magazine.

He reached for his cell phone and brought up her number.

10

CARLY WAS GOING stir crazy.

She'd been cooped up in her apartment for five days, avoiding the paparazzi staked outside her building. After the first couple of days she'd hoped they'd moved on to fresh meat, so she'd ventured out for her usual grande nonfat espresso. The swarm had driven her backward against the front doors.

Lesson learned. So, she'd stayed in. She had plenty to keep her busy. Her blog needed updating. The blog that would never be part of *Modiste* now.

But she dreaded opening her laptop for fear of seeing her father's sordid tale gone viral. The same old footage of his arrest, her mother's too-timely collapse, now with nasty anonymous comments beneath the videos.

Still, she had to leave her apartment sometime. Next week the Mercedes-Benz Fashion Week gala was opening at Lincoln Center to unveil the fall and winter collections and reporting on Fashion Week was essential to her blog's success. She'd get a scoop on the latest trends, note which industry leaders were in attendance, maybe even try to get a photo and quote from the top designers. She absolutely couldn't *not* go. What was her blog without Fashion Week?

Her big fat failure of a blog.

Still, by next week, surely the paparazzi would have found someone new to torture.

Her cell rang and she jumped. Please, not Mother again. She picked it up to check the ID and froze. Her heart thumped against her rib cage. Joe.

She should just let it go to voice mail. She swallowed and hit Answer. "Yes?" Good. Her voice was steady, in control.

There was an instant of silence. "Carly?"

Her breathing hitched at the sound of his deep voice. Had it only been a week since she'd been tangled in the sheets with him? "Joe. Did you need something?"

"I was just checking to see if you were okay."

She blinked. He was worried about her? After the way she'd practically thrown him out of her shower and cabin that last day of the cruise? "I'm fine. Why wouldn't I be?" She winced, squeezed her eyes closed. Defensive much?

Another pause. "I saw your picture in the tabloids. It can't be easy having all that brought up again."

Her throat tightened. When was the last time anyone had cared if she was okay? "I told you, I'm fine."

Another moment of awkward silence. "Did you need anything else?" Good. That should get rid of him. But a part of her ached at the thought.

"I…thought I might come over. Take you to dinner."

She stifled a sigh of relief, of yearning. "Look, Joe. I've been taking care of myself for a long time. I don't need a hero to ride in on his white horse and save me."

She heard an exasperated growl and pictured him running a hand through his hair. Oh, how she remembered that low growl from deep in his throat when he was turned on. She sat and crossed her legs, trying to ease the sharp pang of arousal.

"It's just dinner, Carly, I'm not slaying the kraken."

She couldn't help but smile. Leave it to Joe to reduce a complicated issue to a simple concept. And, oh, how she missed that. Missed smiling. Missed being the carefree woman that only seemed to exist when he was around. She thought it'd just been the atmosphere of the cruise. The flavor of the Bahamas. Yet the moment Joe had left her cabin she'd felt a weight press in on her again.

But that was probably because the cruise had been over and the high from the endorphins from the mind-blowing sex had been wearing off. Maybe they could go to dinner, keep it simple and see where it led? As long as Joe understood it was just for tonight.

"Carly?"

She focused her gaze and realized she hadn't answered. "Dinner?" She couldn't be seen with him in public. The paparazzi would really have a field day with that. She closed her eyes, shook her head. "We can't go out."

"O…kay."

She inhaled. "I mean, I don't want to go out. The cameras, the—"

"Let me take care of it."

"What are you—"

"I'll be there at seven, okay? See you tonight."

"But, Joe!" But he'd already ended the call.

No, TOO DRESSY.

Standing in her bra and tummy-control undies, Carly tossed the padded hanger with the jersey dress onto her bed and strode back to her closet. Shoving aside one outfit after another, she pulled out a silk blouse, held it in front of her and twisted to check it in the mirror. Maybe she should just wear jeans. But she wanted to wear the Ferragamos.

She dropped the hanger with the blouse back on the rod. Why was she obsessing over what to wear? It's not as if she was going to let Joe take her out. She slumped into a chair. Wasn't it obvious? For the same reason she'd spent the entire afternoon waxing and shaving, painting her nails, fixing her hair and applying her makeup just so.

She was an idiot.

An emergency siren blared, sounding as if it were right outside her building. She got up and moved to her window, pulled aside the blinds and peeked out.

A bright red fire truck with lights flashing rolled through the sludge of muddy snow and came to a stop about half a block down the street. Was there a fire somewhere? Or was someone hurt?

As she watched, firemen jumped out of the truck, some racing for the building next door, others pulling out a long hose and another heading for the fire hydrant. Not a good sign.

Then something amazing happened.

Moving as a single entity the paparazzi rushed over to snap pictures of the firemen and the building. The moment they left her stoop, a guy in a heavy winter coat carrying two shopping bags appeared from the opposite direction and jogged up the steps. Just before he disappeared from view, he looked up.

Joe!

Carly grinned. And kept grinning as she danced all the way to her intercom to buzz him into her building. Then she ran back to her bedroom, rethinking her undies. She tore them off and slipped on a thong, some jeans and the silk blouse and raced back to the door. She stood there, her stomach in knots, shifting her weight from foot to foot. Feet! She looked down, groaned, and hurried back to yank off her fuzzy socks and slip on her Kate Spade ankle boots.

Her buzzer rang and she ran back to answer the door. Her trembling hand on the knob, she hesitated. She couldn't catch her breath. This was so dumb. To be so eager over a guy. Really. She wasn't fifteen anymore. Even at fifteen she'd never gone gaga over some dude.

She breathed in. Let it out slowly. Just as a knock sounded on the door, she turned the dead bolt, unlocked the chain and opened it.

And there he was.

Her breath whooshed out of her lungs. No guy had ever made her feel this rush of desire, the overwhelming stimulation to her senses. But something about Joe made her skin tingle. Made her want to throw herself at him. Tear his clothes off, wrap her legs around his waist and—

"Hi." He was smiling and his stubble had thickened to a beard, emphasizing his white teeth. But he still had that clean woodsy fragrance. She made a mental note to ask him the name of his cologne.

She smiled casually. "Hi."

He raised his brows and lifted the two shopping bags to eye level. Her eye level, anyway. "I brought stuff for lasagna."

"Oh." Her mouth watered at the image of home-cooked lasagna. When had she last eaten homemade anything? But she'd expected takeout. Or…she didn't know, but not something so time-consuming. "You cook?"

He grinned as he stepped inside. "Of course. I got the double whammy. I'm Italian *and* I'm a fireman."

"We could've just ordered something."

He looked offended. "No way." Moving past her, he stopped and surveyed her tiny apartment and nodded toward the kitchen area. "With your permission?"

She waved him on, and then shut the door, locking the dead bolt. "Sure."

He shed his coat, tossed it over a barstool, and started unloading the ingredients from the shopping bags. His tight black sweatshirt sported the bright yellow block letters FDNY across his chest.

Joining him at the counter, she fingered the fresh loaf of French bread, the romaine lettuce and ripe tomatoes.

The fresh garlic. "I'd offer to help, but you'd be sorry." She gave him a rueful grin.

"Can you open wine?" He handed her a bottle of 2005 Massolino Barolo. Mmm, impressive. She dug in the drawer for her corkscrew.

"And you could put on some music."

She made herself stop staring. Music. What did she have on her iPod that he would like? As she opened the wine and reached for wineglasses, she mulled over her somewhat eclectic assortment. Heavy metal was out. She didn't think he'd appreciate her opera soundtracks. She poured the wine and then settled for country rock.

Meanwhile Joe had helped himself to her limited number of pots and pans, had water on to boil and meat sizzling on the stove. He was chopping garlic and on-ions and scooping them into a pot of tomato sauce. Her stomach rumbled. When had she last eaten? This morn-ing sometime.

Almost in a daze she moved the laptop, magazines and bills off her tiny table and set out plates and…why not? Candles.

Her stomach rumbled again and she moved to the pot with the sauce. Joe was chopping mushrooms. "How much longer?"

He scowled. "Never rush a good sauce. Look in there." He pointed to the shopping bag with his elbow. "I brought appetizers."

Oddly pleased, Carly grabbed the bag and peeked inside. She threw him a puzzled glance and pulled out an avocado-green plastic container. "What is it?"

He raised his brows. "See for yourself."

She popped the lid and stared at asparagus perfectly wrapped in prosciutto. They were covered with sprinkles of freshly grated parmesan. Her mouth watered. She actually hummed as she licked her lips. "Are you secretly a top chef or something?"

He winced sheepishly. "My mom made those."

The fact that his mother had made food for him should've been a huge red flag. But she pictured the plump woman she'd seen hugging him at the airport, the love for her son radiating from her, and how she'd gone to so much trouble for him tonight.

Her throat tightened as depression hit her.

Geez. What was all this moodiness about? She shook it off.

Besides, at that moment he could've told her Tony Soprano had made them and she would've written the mafia don a personal thank-you note. Grabbing a plate and fork, she served herself, and cut a bite, stuffing it into her mouth. Mmm. She closed her eyes, and maybe swayed on her feet a bit. "Your mother is a goddess," she said after swallowing.

He smiled. "Man, would she love you. We all take her cooking for granted."

Carly fiddled with the knife and fork. A mother's love. Now in her case, there was an oxymoron.

Those onions were stinging her eyes. "So, you have a lot of family?"

He nodded as he chopped mushrooms. "The Tedescos are the reason for the cliché of the big Italian family. Two brothers, two sisters. All older than me, which sucks."

"I don't know…" She shrugged.

"Believe me. You wouldn't say that if you knew what they've put me through over the years. One time, my brother Bernardo and I were altar servers together, and he hid our pet hamster inside the tabernacle—where they keep the Eucharist—and when I opened it during Mass the hamster jumped out and, well, you can imagine the rest."

Carly gasped. "That's awful!"

"It's okay." Joe grinned. "I got even eventually."

"How?"

"By the time I was in ninth grade, I was half a foot taller than Bernie. I never let him forget it. And I never had to wear his hand-me-downs again."

Carly shuddered. "You're right. I'm glad I'm an only child." She looked up from taking another bite and got caught in his dark gaze.

"Still, it must be nice to not be so…alone."

His smile faded. Had she said that out loud? What was that look in his eyes? Sympathy? Whatever it was, it was too intense. She cut another bite of the asparagus and held the fork to his mouth.

With both hands full of mushroom pieces, he opened his mouth and angled his chin to catch all the asparagus. But his gaze never left hers. As he chewed, his eyes heated, staring into hers. Was he remembering all the things they'd done together in that cruise-ship cabin? Suddenly she wanted to postpone dinner and lead him to her bedroom.

"How long does that sauce have to simmer?" Her voice sounded husky. She laid her palm on his chest.

His brown eyes flared, darkened, the color of espresso. His gaze dropped to her mouth and his head lowered. His lips parted. He had such full sensual lips. He dropped the mushrooms to the counter, cradled her head and brought those lips to hers.

His kiss was deep and powerful, full of hunger. She reached up and circled her arms around his neck, clinging to him. She'd missed this. Missed his passion, his strength, the way he could make her feel as if she was the only person on the planet he wanted to be with.

His fingers raked through her hair, angling her head. And his tongue swept in, devastating her mouth, demanding her response. His hands slid down to the small of her back, one to rest on her butt. He held her tight and a low groan rumbled in his throat.

One minute he was kissing her, the next he gripped her wrists, pulled her hands away from his neck and stepped back.

Carly blinked. What the—

Joe just stood there, breathing hard, his eyes closed. Without a word, he turned away, scooped the mushrooms into the pot. Dusting his hands, he took a cooking spoon and began to mix them in. "The sauce has to be stirred constantly."

Carly had to regroup. What had just happened here? He didn't want…? Then why had he come over? For the sparkling conversation? She didn't know what to make of him. Was he trying to be Mr. Sensitive? Or did he think she required some form of intimacy before they'd have sex? Uh, that ship had sailed. Literally. Maybe he was just trying to build up anticipation.

Whatever his reason, she wanted him in her bed.

He cleared his throat. "So, I looked at your blog. It's a pretty cool concept. How'd you get into that?"

Really? Was he serious? It appeared he wanted to… talk.

11

"How'd I get into fashion? Or how'd I get into blogging?"

Joe shrugged. "Either one. Both." He stared into the saucepan, gripping the spoon like an erupting water hose when what he really wanted to do was take Carly in his arms, kiss her until she couldn't think and carry her to her bed.

But as much as he'd enjoyed their time on the cruise, he'd ended up feeling like her boy toy. A shipboard distraction she could discard and forget. He wasn't going to settle for simply being a convenient booty call. Even if he had called her.

Carly picked up her glass of wine and moved to sit on the stool at the bar. "I've always loved fashion." A corner of her soft pink mouth curled up in a reminiscent smile. "I think my first words were *haute couture*." She sipped her wine. "Some of my earliest memories are of my mother dressing to go out. She'd always ask me which dress she should wear. I'd always help her choose her shoes and jewelry. When most girls were playing dress up I was copying famous designers' outfits for myself. Sitting in some designer's studio while my mother shopped was better than Christmas and my birthday combined."

Whoa. Even when he'd eaten, breathed and slept football in high school the sport had never been better than Christmas. Or his birthday. Or sex.

"I think—" she stared into the distance, pensive "—dressing well is like wearing armor." She blinked, refocused on him and shook her head. "That sounds crazy, doesn't it?"

"No."

She cocked her head and something flickered in her eyes, and then was gone before he could identify it. "Anyway, I always had good instincts for style. I love manipulating fabrics and designs to enhance a figure and achieve the optimal silhouette."

He could believe it. She did seem to have an eye for the perfect outfit for each occasion. Take tonight, for instance. The neckline of her silky pink shirt draped between her breasts, and he fought to keep his gaze from drifting to the hint of creamy, rounded flesh. For some reason that was sexier than if she was standing in front of him stark naked.

Whoa. He had to stop his thoughts from wandering to that image of Carly, otherwise he'd be in big trouble. As he stirred the sauce he tried to think of something interesting to say. *Her eyes are up there, Tedesco!*

He met her gaze.

One of her brows arched skeptically and she placed

her folded arms on the bar in front of her and leaned in. "You sure you have to keep stirring that sauce?"

No. No, he wasn't. "Yeah. It just doesn't taste the same if you don't."

She stared at him with those penetrating, almost-silver blue eyes, and then gave a tiny shrug.

Was he really going to resist her? "So, what about the blog?"

She grimaced. "That's a long story."

"I got nothing but time." With a smile, he transferred his attention from her to the sauce again.

She busied herself with pouring more wine. "After my father…" One delicate shoulder lifted. "One of my part-time jobs was in a department store, and the more I helped women choose their clothing, I began to realize that although fashion magazines might have an article every so often about how to dress to flatter different body types, there was nothing instantly available where a woman could find such information. She was dependent upon the expertise—or lack thereof—of the salesperson." When Carly paused to sip her wine, he watched her delicate throat as she swallowed and then followed her tongue as it licked her glistening lips.

Okay, that wasn't helping the problem.

"You said, *one* of your part-time jobs? How many did you have?" He concentrated on opening the pasta and dropping it in the boiling water.

"Two during college, at first, then I was able to get full-time at the apparel factory at night, and quit one of my part-time jobs."

Joe whistled under his breath. Just looking at her,

one wouldn't know how tough she really was. "Where'd you graduate?"

"NYU." She snuck another bite of the asparagus.

"When did you start the blog?"

"I thought only the police were allowed to interrogate suspects."

"Indulge me. I'm making you dinner."

"Ah, that's how it is, is it?" She sighed. "I took a computer class, learned all about web design and voila, *Carly's Couture.*"

"So, how does it work? You endorse merchandise from the large department stores and in return they advertise with you?" Joe added the drained meat to the sauce.

"Sometimes. I also might recommend an item from a secondhand shop or a vintage store. It just depends. The important thing is my suggestions are free for the average woman or man, and I'm able to support myself."

"And how do you know what to recommend?"

"Each woman is unique. Her skin tone, the shape of her face, her coloring. The best feature of the blog is the interactive part where a person can enter their dimensions, click on their face shape, hair color, eye color, etcetera, and then I generate a personalized style just for them. I even take their personality and profession into account in deciding what fashions and accessories suit their unique lifestyle. And I write a daily blog about fresh trends, where to find sales, even hair and makeup tips."

The more she talked about her blog, the more animated she became. But not in a manic way, like his family got when the dinnertime discussions got overheated or downright crazed, everyone trying to outyell the other. Hers was more of a refined enthusiasm, a graceful passion. Her face flushed. Her eyes sparkled. Her voice lifted. Passion looked good on her.

She leaned back, crossed her legs. "What about you? Did you run around pretending to be a fireman as a kid?" She sipped her wine.

"Me? Nah, I wanted to be a football player." He rummaged for a colander and set it in the sink. "Great game, '91 championship. I was eight."

"The Giants against the Buffalo Bills!" She half stood, her face lighting up.

"Wow, you couldn't have been more than four or five and you remember that?"

"Well, I know my Giants!"

He nodded, impressed. "I remember watching that game with my dad and my brothers. The Buffalo Bills trying to score that field goal at the last minute. And we all went berserk when the Giants won."

"Twenty to nineteen, right? And Ottis Anderson rushing 102 yards!"

"That's right. Simms was out with an injury and Hostetler quarterbacked that game! You *do* know your Giants." This was a side of Carly he'd never have suspected. And he liked it.

"I never miss a game. On Sunday, you should come—" the excitement vanished in her expression "—over and watch."

He stared at her. What? She regretted inviting him all of a sudden? Maybe he should give her an easy out.

He could always just say he only watched if the Giants played. Grabbing some oven mitts, he lifted the pot of pasta and dumped it, draining the hot water.

But he wanted to see her again.

And over the past week he'd found himself unable to let it go. He wanted more than just a pleasant interlude during a fun vacation. The woman intrigued him. She was complicated. And damned if he didn't like that about her.

If he'd been going to settle down with a nice girl from St. Cecilia's, he'd had plenty of opportunities. His sisters had fixed him up dozens of times over the years. Even Father Lionel had slipped him a phone number or two. He'd eventually ask the girl out, maybe even try a second date. But there was no interest. No…spark.

So, he wanted to see where this would lead. He already knew the sex was amazing.

"I'd like that." He nodded, then handed her the rectangular casserole dish. "You want to help me layer the ingredients?"

WHILE THEY ATE Joe talked about the Giants. He'd played football in high school—a tight end. Of course he'd been a jock. He had that build. Broad shoulders. Long, muscular legs. And a tight end. She smiled to herself. Suppressed a giggle.

Too many glasses of wine, Carly!

Or not enough sex.

She set her glass down and focused on Joe. Was he talking about the other firemen, and their wives and children, or his own family? All the people in his life seemed to intermingle as he talked about getting together at each other's houses for cookouts and to watch the games.

She blinked as her mind conjured up an image of him in his football uniform, the pants fitting snugly across his butt as he bent over to huddle with his teammates. Mmm…

Concentrate, Carly.

Nieces, nephews, Brooklyn. Did his eyes always twinkle like that? And his voluptuous lips. Voluptuous? She set the wine aside.

Speaking of, the way he sat with his long legs spread wide just begged one's gaze to admire his, uh, endowments. Well, she couldn't help if it was a clear glass table, could she?

She looked up into his eyes. What had he been saying? Was he waiting on her to reply?

"I'm sorry, what?"

"So you don't have any brothers or sisters?"

"No, it's just me. Thank goodness." She tried to smile then looked away.

Frowning, he sat back, gave her a calculating look. "With four siblings, I can't even imagine what that would be like. But it sounds lonely."

Lonely? Desolate, more like. She'd been naturally quiet anyway, but growing up in the huge house with her parents gone most of the day, she'd spent hours on her computer. She remembered begging her mother for a baby brother or sister. One time she'd even tried to conjure up an imaginary friend. No luck.

But those hours on the PC had paid off eventually.

He glanced around her tiny apartment. "I notice you don't have any photos of your family. Is your mom still living?"

"We don't need to talk about my family." She stood and walked around the table, never dropping her gaze. "We don't need to talk anymore at all, do we?" Taking his hand, she pulled him to his feet. He stood willingly enough and she rose on tiptoe to cover his mouth with hers.

Mmm, his kiss was tangy and sweet. And skillful. This time he had nothing to slice or chop. No sauce to stir. She'd waited long enough. She needed him naked. Now.

He tried to pull away, but his lips didn't go far. His eyes held conflict, part smoldering heat and part reluctance.

"Joe." His name came out as a whispered plea. She curled her fingers under the hem of his sweatshirt and lifted it over his firm chest, tugging it off when he helpfully raised his arms. His mouth came back to hers as soon as she'd removed his shirt, and when it returned he took the kiss deeper, stronger.

Yes.

She walked him backward toward her bedroom, enjoying the hot flesh under her hands. When she ran her palms over his nipples he groaned and pulled her tight against him. Thankfully the bed was close and when he bumped into the frame he stumbled and fell onto the mattress. She followed him down and straddled his thighs, unbuttoning his jeans and dragging kisses down his flat stomach as she carefully unzipped him.

Before he could stop her she had him in her mouth, drawing on his length with strong, determined strokes. "Ah, Carly." He gasped and muttered something about saints, then lifted his hips to match her rhythm.

She relished his taste as she ran her tongue around and over the tip. She relished his moans and the fingers he smoothed through her hair. And she especially relished when he squeezed her shoulders and brought her up and over him.

"That's enough of that unless you want this to end right now." He rolled her beneath him and took charge of undressing her, starting with her blouse, which she helped unbutton and pull off her arms. But he got distracted when he unhooked her bra and tossed it somewhere behind him.

The look in his eyes as he stared at her was a mix of admiration and desire. Joe smiled and kissed his way across both breasts, and then suckled one deeply before moving to the other.

His body radiated heat. For the first time since she'd returned to New York she felt warm again. Her life was cold, empty. But all he'd had to do was step into her apartment and everything seemed different, brighter.

Not wanting to give that any thought, she called out for more as he lapped at each sensitive peak. She couldn't wait much longer. Patience had never been a virtue of hers. She wanted him inside her. "Joe."

"Hmm?" He moved his mouth down to her stomach, trailing kisses as he went. She quickly got rid of her jeans and thong, anxious for him to resume where he'd left off.

"There're condoms in the bedside drawer."

"Okay." But he didn't move to get them. He kissed the ticklish spot just below her hip bone and then nuzzled between her thighs. His beard added a delicious friction.

She arched off the mattress and whatever she'd been worrying about was completely forgotten as an aching pleasure wound through every artery and vein.

But she didn't want to climax this way. "Joe, wait." She sat up and cupped his face. "Wait."

He stopped, lifted his gaze to hers, his expression concerned. "What's wrong?"

I want to feel you inside me when I come. I want your arms around me. I want to see your eyes. I want us to come together. But all she said was, "I want you. Now."

Her clit still throbbed as he caressed her and then thrust inside her in one beautiful, satisfying stroke. After that the room disappeared.

All she could see were the strands of his black hair that curled so adoringly over his forehead, the warmth in his eyes as he gazed into hers. All she could hear were his murmurs of approval. All she could feel was the way his hands clung to hers, silently promising he wouldn't leave her alone. In that moment he became her world.

He kissed her breasts, her jaw, her mouth and his pace sped up. The faster strokes did her in. She cried out as she came and he buried his nose into her neck and stiffened and shuddered.

It was a long while before she floated back to reality. Joe was placing tiny kisses along her temple to her forehead. And she was stroking her fingers through the hair at his nape. He didn't move off her. And she didn't want him to. If only they could stay like this forever. Where all her troubles seemed so far away, and even if they dared show up, she was safe in Joe's big strong arms.

"Oh, man." Joe brought his mouth to hers, his kiss intense, full of purpose. When he lifted his head, how he looked at her. His eyes were serious, with a hint of wonder. "I've missed this."

So had she.

Drawing in a deep breath, he rolled to his back and let out a heavy sigh.

Carly felt as limp as the pasta they'd boiled for tonight's meal. Lazily, she rolled to curl against Joe's side, throwing her leg over both of his as she ran her hand down his chest, noting every hard plane and ripple.

It'd been as if they'd never missed a beat since the cruise. She'd told herself the earth-shattering sex was attributable to the newness of her lover. Like wearing a new outfit for the first time, Joe had been exciting and different. But, unlike a new outfit, sex with him just got better each time they came together.

He rubbed her back while he gazed about her room. "You keep surprising me."

She smiled. "I aim to please." She nestled her cheek closer to his left nipple.

With a quick laugh, he gave her a playful swat on her backside. "No, I mean, like, your bedroom, for instance. It's nice, but simple. It's not all designer furniture and postmodern whatever."

Carly glanced around her bedroom, trying to see it

through his eyes. It was a mess. "I didn't have much time to straighten up after you called."

"No, it's not that. You don't know messy until you've seen my place. I mean, the whole vibe is different."

Vibe? True, she hadn't refurnished this room after her blog started taking off. Buying the new pieces in her living room and kitchen had been a priority. But it hadn't seemed important to spend money on her bedroom. Now she realized that even though she had the money, she liked these used pieces from her college days. They were comfortable.

She shrugged, not wanting to think about any deeper meaning behind her choice.

"And you don't seem like the kind of woman who likes to watch football."

"Just because I love haute couture I can't love football?"

The hand rubbing her back stilled. "Now, I didn't say that. But you have to admit that the two don't exactly go together."

"I suppose." She grinned and lifted her head to raise a brow at him. "What can I say, I'm just exceptional."

She expected him to scoff, or laugh, or accuse her of egotism. But his eyes turned serious. "You are."

Her smile faded. How did she respond to that?

Luckily, he switched to their original topic. "How'd you get into football?"

"My dad." Memories snuck into her contented afterglow.

Watching the games with her father had been the only time he'd spent with her. Or rather, she spent with him. He'd always told her she was Daddy's Little Darling—and hadn't her mother thrown that accusation at her enough? But the truth was her daddy was rarely home. And even when he was all she usually got was a quick "How was your day?".

She blinked, coming back to the present. "When he wasn't at work, he'd be in his study watching football. I'd take the tray of snacks from the maid and bring it in to him so we could watch together. Over the years I learned everything I could about the game."

Ridiculous now, to think how she had cherished those times.

If only people knew how insignificant she was to her father, they might not be so quick to believe that she'd known about his crimes.

Joe turned to face her, tightening his arms around her. "Whoa, you just went somewhere dark. Were you thinking about your dad?"

"What?" She looked into his eyes and saw pity there. Wait. He felt sorry for her because her father was a crook? Her breath caught. Maybe he did think, like everyone else, that she had to have known about her father's scam. Just the notion that he might believe that was like a stab through her heart.

Shoving out of his arms, she scooted to the edge of the mattress. "You know, it's getting kind of late."

"Excuse me?" Joe sat up, running a hand through his hair. She could feel his gaze on her, hear the confusion in his voice.

She couldn't help that.

He'd done it again. Gotten her all relaxed and sated

and then, bam, gone for the jugular. Asking her questions, making her remember things.

She stood and padded to the bathroom. Before she could shut the door, he followed her, reached up and gripped each side of the door frame. "What just happened here?"

"What do you mean?" She clung to the doorknob, hoping he'd take the hint and go. Just because he caught her in a weak moment and she'd talked about her father, he thought that meant she was going to get all soft and mushy now?

His expression hardened. "Man, you are some piece of work. You got what you wanted and now I can go, is that it?"

She scoffed. "Don't pretend there was some other reason you came over here tonight."

His jaw dropped. "Wow. How cynical can you be?" He pushed off the door frame and strode across the room to scoop up his jeans and underwear off the floor. "And here I was worrying about you," he muttered as he shoved his legs into his jeans.

"I don't need you to worry. I'm fine."

"You're right. Why did I bother?" He shook his head as he found his boots and tugged them on. "I must be the world's stupidest average Joe."

During his tirade, Carly grabbed her robe off the door hook and slipped it on. She followed him out to the kitchen, fighting a crazy desire to apologize, to ask him to come back to bed. She'd even promise to snuggle with him and make him breakfast in the morning. Whatever he wanted.

But this was for the best. "So, thanks for dinner."

Clamping his lips together, he strode to the front door, unlocked the dead bolt and swung it open. Then he faced her. "Have a nice life," he told her and slammed the door behind him.

Carly spied his coat still slung over the stool and almost ran after him to return it. It was freezing out there. Instead she left it out in the hallway.

This was just as well. At least she didn't have to worry about how to get out of that date. She'd regretted the invitation to watch the game together the minute she heard the words escape her mouth. She didn't want him thinking nights like tonight were going to be a regular thing between them. Her time should be spent on her blog, figuring out how to capitalize on the contest now that *Modiste* had backed out.

Besides, the guy might as well be wearing a T-shirt that announced he was looking for a house in a borough, a wife and 2.5 kids. And that was the last thing she wanted.

Wasn't it?

12

DESPITE THREE AND a half feet of snow on the ground, and more expected before morning, O'Malley's was packed. As soon as Joe walked in, his buddies waved him over. He stomped the slush off his boots and shrugged out of his coat—his lighter-weight coat—then grabbed a stool at the bar next to Wakowski.

"Did I miss any wardrobe malfunctions?" Joe gestured to the bartender for a beer and focused on the big screen mounted in the corner.

"Nah, it's still the first quarter. But there were a couple of good commercials." Wakowski tossed some peanuts in his mouth.

Ah, the big game. It just didn't get any better than this. After coming off a twenty-four-hour shift this morning, this was just what he needed.

"Hey, what'd your ma make today?" Wakowski asked between munching.

"How'd you know I went there?"

"Come on. It's Sunday, ain't it?"

Joe grinned. "Chicken cacciatore."

"Aw, geez. And you didn't bring me any?"

"It's out in the car. Your wife burn supper again?"

Wakowski lifted his gaze to the ceiling. "Burning it would be more merciful, you know what I'm sayin'?"

Joe chuckled. Wakowski had been complaining about his wife's cooking ever since Joe had met the guy ten years ago, back when Joe was a rookie fireman. But all the guys knew Wakowski was crazy about his wife even if she was a lousy cook. He lived for her and their five kids.

When the bartender set his beer before him, Joe raised his bottle. "To the first responders!"

Every man and woman cheered and raised their glasses, followed by a brief moment of silence. O'Malley's was the local watering hole for Engine 288. One wall held nothing but eight by tens of every fire-fighter who'd lost his or her life on 9/11.

Joe grabbed a handful of pretzels and settled in to watch what was left of the game. Was Carly watching, too? Was she alone? Or did she have friends she watched the game with? Or maybe some other guy?

Thinking about her with some other guy raised his blood pressure. It shouldn't. She'd made it more than clear on the cruise ship that he was nothing more to her than a quick, good time. And yet he'd come back for more. He must be one sandwich short of a picnic. Had he actually worried about her? He'd even gone so far as to think they might…what? Date? Have a relationship?

He'd given the exercise equipment at the station a thorough workout the past two days trying to burn off the frustration. He'd even called one of the girls his sisters had been trying to fix him up with and made a date for next weekend.

O'Malley's patrons erupted in a thunderous cheer and Joe snapped out of his wandering thoughts. His team had scored a touchdown and he'd missed it.

He needed to stop thinking about her. To that end, he scanned the pub for interesting females. The bleached blonde was a no. The redhead was too young. A pretty brunette in the corner was sizing him up. But she seemed too eager. Wiggling her fingers in a cutesy wave, nodding at him every time he caught her eye.

He could hear his ma now. *Find a nice girl. Settle down.*

Carly wasn't nice. Her prickly personality practically dared him to try to get closer. But that was part of that spark, wasn't it?

He was doing it again, thinking about her. He sipped his beer and tried to concentrate on the game. This kind of day used to be what it was all about. Surrounded by good friends, in his favorite pub, watching his favorite sport.

His cell vibrated against his hip and he pulled it out to check caller ID. Probably his ma making sure he'd—

Carly?

He almost didn't answer. He shouldn't.

Mumbling a swear word his ma would smack him for, he thumbed the answer button. "What?"

She said something, but he could barely hear her. He slid off the stool to head into the vestibule. "Just a sec, let me get where I can hear." He stepped out to the bar's foyer. "What is it?"

"Where are you?"

He stuck his free hand in his pocket. Did it matter? "O'Malley's Bar and Grill. What do you need?"

"I thought you might come over and watch the game with me."

"Look, Carly. I can't be the guy you call when you want some."

Silence.

"Carly?"

"My dad couldn't have cared less that I learned about football to be close to him. He barely knew I was alive. My mother lives in New Mexico with her third husband and only calls when she wants something, and yes, being only child was lonely. I'm still lonely. I don't have any friends and I know people think I'm a cold witch. I wouldn't know what to do with a friend if I had one, and I know I was horrible to you, but…I don't want to be alone today."

Joe stood frozen between the outer doors and the inner doors. He couldn't believe she was telling him all this.

"Joe? Will you…will you come over and watch the game with me?"

For the third time in less than an hour he thought about what he shouldn't do regarding Carly. He shouldn't go over there.

Aw, who was he kidding?

"Give me half an hour."

AFTER TWO DAYS away from him, barely thinking about him more than once or twice a day, okay, maybe more than that, Carly thought she'd exaggerated in her mind how much just being around him intoxicated her. But when he rang her intercom, and she heard his voice, her stomach twisted and her breathing quickened. And worst of all, her hands actually shook as she buzzed him in.

Willing her nerves to calm, she opened the door.

Unwinding a knitted scarf from around his neck, Joe pointed his thumb behind him. "Lucky for me they're shooting a film a few blocks over."

"Oh, yeah, I should've let you know the paparazzi found a new victim." She stood awkwardly staring at him. So handsome the back of her throat ached. He managed to make a pair of worn, dark brown corduroys and a forest-green cable-knit sweater look as if they belonged on the cover of *GQ*.

He cleared his throat and she snapped to attention. "Oh, sorry. Come in." She widened the door opening and stepped back, wiping her hands on her jeans. "I didn't know if you'd eaten, so I ordered Indian, just in case." She gestured toward the white, square, takeout boxes on the coffee table.

His eyes widened as they fixed on the food. Then he shrugged. "I could eat." He strode to the sofa, shedding the lightweight jacket and tossing it across the club chair. The same chair that held his heavy coat.

"Have a seat." She gestured at the couch. "You want a beer?"

"Sure." He plopped down, then draped his arm

across the back of the sofa and glanced at her, his expression wary.

Her chest tightened, now she was the one confused.

How could one vulnerable look from this easygoing guy make her feel anxious and insecure? Not even the editor at *Modiste* had managed to do that.

While he made himself comfortable, she stepped into the kitchen and grabbed a couple of beers from the fridge. "Halftime's about to start." Curling a leg beneath her, she joined him on the sofa, setting a plate, fork and beer in front of him.

Though she rarely watched television outside of football and Project Runway, she was glad now that she'd splurged on the forty-inch flat-screen. She grabbed the remote and turned up the volume. But she felt his stare prickling her skin. She turned her head and got caught in his dark brown eyes.

He was looking at her so intensely, his gaze so serious.

She licked her lips. "What?"

He smiled, the corners of his eyes crinkling, his teeth flashing. "You're nervous. Is this such a scary prospect?"

She scowled, leaned away, crossed her arms. "Why would I be scared?"

The hand resting along the sofa lifted to tuck a strand of her hair behind her ear. "I think the idea of dropping your tough-gal attitude and opening up to someone frightens you. But that's okay. I'm scared, too." He inched closer, staring into her eyes. "Why do you have to be so damn tempting?" With a groan he cupped the sides of her head and covered her mouth.

At first his kiss was soft, persuasive. Then he circled his arms around her waist and pulled her close, opening his lips to drink her in.

She was so confused. So, he *did* want sex? That, she could do.

With a moan, she lay back on the sofa and pulled him down with her, pushing her breasts against his powerful chest. She loved how he felt in her arms. The strain of his hard back and shoulder muscles beneath her palms, the intense heat that warmed her, when she could never get warm on her own.

She sighed, lost in his kisses. He moved his lips down to her jaw, her neck, below her ear. She wanted more. Slipping a hand between them, she cupped him through his jeans.

He made a strangled sound and lifted off her.

It took her a moment to come out of her lust-filled haze. Her body pulsed and ached. There was a void that needed filling. She sat up slowly, straightening her cashmere cardigan. "What's the matter?"

"Nothing, I…" He cleared his throat. "I know I came here to watch the game, but I couldn't resist kissing you. I just got carried away." He pointed at the TV. "I liked her latest album." With an arm around her shoulders, he tugged her close and gave the show his complete attention.

Carly blinked. She stared at him while he seemed absorbed in watching the award-winning singer belt out her chart-topping hit. Frustration ignited into resentment. Was he teasing her on purpose? Hadn't she groveled enough?

But she'd rather have him here than go through what she'd experienced the past couple of days. In his company, she felt as if she mattered to someone. Felt as if he accepted her prickly, difficult nature—liked it, even. Funny how she'd become spoiled to that feeling in just a short time around him.

Which was terrifying. What happened when he moved on? He probably made everyone he met feel that way. He'd even managed to charm the petulant Piper. Best not get too accustomed to having him around. He wouldn't put up with her prickliness forever. But she'd enjoy it while it lasted, knowing there was an expiration date. With a safety net in place, so to speak, she relaxed and concentrated on enjoying the evening.

The halftime show ended and the sports commentators began their rundown. Joe sat back, one ankle crossed over the other knee. He helped himself to some of the chicken malai kabob and sipped his beer.

Making a plate of food for herself, Carly settled against his side, ate and watched the game. She tried to work up an enthusiasm for the yards gained, the touchdowns, who was winning, but the truth was, she mainly noticed how Joe's body fit around hers, how his fingers rubbed up and down her arm, how he would absentmindedly brush his lips across her temple while keeping his gaze on the television.

Large snowflakes floated past her window, falling heavier as the night grew later. She drew her wooly blanket up over her legs and snuggled deeper against Joe.

He tightened his arm around her and looked down at her. "You cold?"

Gazing up into his eyes, she melted and barely managed a quick nod.

"Can't have that." He slid an arm beneath her and hauled her up onto his lap, circling his arms around her.

Her eyes watered. She slid her hands behind his back and nuzzled her cold nose into his neck.

"Aw, Carly. What am I going to do with you?" He sighed, and then shifted one arm beneath her knees, lifted her as he got to his feet and carried her to her bedroom.

13

GOOD THING HE hadn't adopted a dog like he'd been thinking he might.

Joe had been back to his apartment exactly once since he left O'Malley's. And even then it was only to grab a change of clothes. The rest of the time he stayed at Carly's. Mostly they were wrapped in each other's arms under her down comforter.

Starvation finally forced them out sometime Monday evening. They ended up at a deli she liked, slugging through the dirty snow until they snagged a cab. But the rest of the time they stayed in, ordered takeout and found a lot of interesting places in her apartment to make love.

Still, it wasn't just the sex he loved. He discovered he could talk to Carly. They discussed everything from football to politics to international events. She never lacked for an opinion or a unique take on a subject. He found himself considering things he'd never given much thought to before. And even changing his mind about a couple of issues. She'd have made a great public speaker. But she listened to his opinions, too.

By Tuesday night, he was packing his things to head home. He had to be at the firehouse for his shift tomorrow morning. Carly was in the shower. He could already feel her distancing herself from him. As if, now that he had to leave, their fun was over and that's all there'd ever be. Would it be like the end of the cruise all over again?

He heard the water turn off and the shower curtain pull back. Stuffing the last of his clothes in his duffel, he opened the door and leaned against the frame, planning on enjoying the view. When she stepped out, he wasn't disappointed.

He folded his arms to keep from pulling her close and taking her to bed. Again. He wouldn't have thought he'd want her this soon, but where she was concerned, he couldn't seem to get enough. Unfortunately, if he wanted to get any sleep before his shift, he should leave right now.

She smiled at him, kind of a sad smile, then pulled a fluffy towel off the bar and wrapped it around her body, tucking a corner in at the top. "I wish you didn't have to go tonight."

"Unless we get called to a big fire I'll be back Thursday after my shift."

With a grimace, she padded to the sink and grabbed a hairbrush. "I won't be here."

"Where are you going?" Irritation sparked. Was she trying to get rid of him again? He pictured her on another cruise, with another guy, which was crazy. He'd never felt jealous before, not even with Lydia.

"Thursday is the beginning of Fashion Week. I'll be making the rounds from dawn to dawn." She vigorously brushed her hair.

"Oh." Of course. She had to work. Even on the day they'd barely left her bed she'd managed to haul her laptop onto the mattress in the wee hours of the morning and type a new post and answer readers' questions.

So, she wasn't trying to get rid of him. He had plenty of things to keep him busy the next week. Things he'd neglected while he was here. He just couldn't think of anything he wanted to do more than spend time with her.

"So, what happens during Fashion Week?" He moved into the bathroom and leaned against the counter.

"Well, everybody who's anybody will have runway shows previewing their fall-winter collections." She smeared cream on her face and rubbed it in. "That's mostly in the afternoons and evenings. In the mornings the press can get into designers' studios. And after the runway shows there are always parties to attend."

"Sounds exhausting."

She spun to face him. "It is. But it's the most exciting week of the year until the spring-summer previews in September." Next she squirted lotion on her arms and shoulders. He'd never watched a woman's after-shower routine before. Who knew they used so much stuff?

"If I'm lucky I'll get to be in the vicinity of one or two of the really popular designers and maybe get a scoop on a new trend."

"Won't the magazine get you interviews?"

She shook her head, her expression confused. "*Modiste?* Why would they do that?"

"I thought they were sponsoring your blog?"

"No."

"Oh." He had to rethink what he thought he understood about Carly's work. "You mean your blog isn't normally associated with the magazine?"

"No. It's my blog. The magazine only sponsored the contest."

"But why would they do that? Don't they have their own online presence?"

"Yes, but my blog has been very successful. As a matter of fact—" She set the lotion on the counter, a frown forming on her luscious lips.

"What?"

Staring at her hands, she hesitated. "They had talked about bringing *Carly's Couture* in-house."

He was impressed. "That's great. Isn't it?"

She bit her lip, then raised her chin and met his gaze. "They decided to go in a different direction."

Hold on a sec. How long had she known this? "Be… cause of the Piper scandal?"

Her lips thinned and she averted her gaze. "Kind of."

What wasn't she saying? Then it hit him. He jumped to his feet and put an arm around her shoulders. "Because of the scandal with your dad resurfacing?"

She maneuvered out of his hold. "It's no big deal." Grabbing a hair dryer, she turned it on, brushing out her long hair as she dried it.

Yeah, and he was the king of Brooklyn.

He refused to let her pretend this wasn't important to her. Gripping the hair dryer, he turned it off and set it down, then took her by the shoulders.

"What are you doing?" Her eyes were focused on his reflection in the mirror.

"Carly. I think it *was* a big deal. And I'm sorry."

Something flickered in her eyes. Pain she quickly disguised. And replaced with heat. They held a clear message, scorching him. She reached up and dropped the towel.

He checked his watch. It was already late. And he had to be at the station at five…

Forget about it. He'd gone without sleep plenty of times. He yanked his shirt over his head, tossed it somewhere behind him and scooped her up.

"EMILY!" CARLY CALLED to her friend across the busy studio. Okay, Emily wasn't a friend, exactly. More like a professional acquaintance. She was a buyer for Savoy's department store and she sometimes gave Carly inside information on what was going to be really hot in the coming season.

Emily stopped with her hand on the doorknob and spun just as she was leaving. "Oh. Carly. I didn't see you." She smiled but it was only perfunctory.

So, she'd seen the tabloids. Of course she had.

"Hey, what are you excited about in this designer's fall-winter collection this year?"

"I really couldn't say." Emily winced. "Hasn't…Don contacted you?"

Oh, no, no, no. Don was the regional director of marketing for Savoy's. He was supposed to renew the contract for advertising on her blog next month. It stood to reason if *Modiste* didn't want to be associated with Swindleton Pendleton, neither would any of the major department stores.

Panic flared for a moment, but Carly forced warmth into her smile. "Not yet. But I've been out of town, so…" She nodded. "Okay, well, thanks." She had to get somewhere private.

"Hey." Emily caught her arm as she tried to brush past. "Is that hunky fireman around?"

"My contest winner? No, why?"

Emily pouted. "Too bad. Everyone wants to meet him." She leaned in conspiratorially. "I heard he's getting offers from several modeling agencies. He's all the buzz with the designers. Do you know if he's signed with anyone yet?"

Carly stood stunned. Joe hadn't told her about any offers. But she managed a sympathetic smile. "I'm not at liberty to say." As she followed Emily to the elevator, a pang hit her in the vicinity of her chest. Joe had kept the agency offers a secret from her.

Once inside the packed elevator, she backed into a corner and folded her arms. Why hadn't Joe even mentioned it? Did he think she'd be upset? On the contrary, the more popular he became the better for her blog.

After he left Wednesday morning, she'd made coffee and curled up on the sofa. His scent had lingered in the fabric, taunting her with his absence. How lifeless her small apartment had seemed. His presence haunted the place. Which was crazy. She'd always valued her privacy. Hadn't living with Reese taught her she was better off alone?

But she missed Joe.

The elevator doors swished open and she followed the throng out to the freezing, wet street. Hitching her bag higher on her shoulder, she tried to hail a cab, but ended up walking a block before a vacant one stopped.

As she hopped into the back, she gave the driver the address then pulled out her cell and almost punched in Joe's number. He was off today. Maybe she'd meet him for lunch after this next stage show. He could tell her how his shift at the station went. Had he been called to any major fires? She hadn't heard of any big ones on last night's or this morning's local news. She could ask him about the agency offers. If he confirmed them, she could make the news her blog entry tomorrow.

What was she thinking? If he'd wanted her to know, he would've told her. Besides, it'd barely been thirty hours since she saw him. He had his life. She had hers. They didn't have to live in each other's pockets.

But the fashion world evidently thought they did.

When she presented her ticket into the Michaela design studio the next day, she was reluctantly let in, but one would think she'd contracted the Ebola virus the way everyone avoided her. Then, just as she was leaving, an assistant editor at *Madame Claudette* magazine cornered her to ask about Joe. The editor hinted that if he were with Carly they'd surely get invited to the exclusive post-runway party.

Carly seethed. She should've set Emily straight about Joe, but no, she'd just had to throw out that last smug comment, making it seem as if she had inside information on the man.

The last straw came that night, just before the runway show she was attending. The theater was crowded, everyone pressed elbow to elbow, and bulbs were flashing. Carly could feel a migraine building pressure in her temples and behind her eyes.

A young man in a finely tailored suit pushed through the mob to grab her hand and shake it. "Ms. Pendleton? I'm Cam Laughtry, with Franklin Modeling Agency. I hear you're the one to talk to about Joe Tedesco?"

"Me?"

He playfully tapped her forearm with his brochure. "Now, don't act coy." Two invitations for the following morning's private studio gathering appeared from his suit coat. He waved them under her nose. "You bring that sexy Average Joe with you tomorrow, girlfriend, and I'll make it worth your while."

"But he doesn't have any event tickets. They sold out months ago."

"I'll have a set of tickets for the week's events couriered over tonight. You just bring him tomorrow." He winked and sauntered off.

Carly smiled through gritted teeth and found her seat for the runway show. She opened her tablet and took notes during the show, but her usual enthusiasm for the fabulous outfits was crushed. As soon as it ended she hurried down Lincoln Center's grand staircase. It's not as though she would get invited backstage tonight, or to the party afterward.

Not without Joe.

Once in the lobby, she rushed to the restroom and paced the foyer. A woman applying lipstick glanced at her warily in the mirror's reflection, but Carly ignored her.

The idea of needing Joe to snag an interview or get into parties infuriated her. She'd spent years making her blog the success it was today. Years of working two jobs, of sacrifice and long hours to build a name and a successful business. And now her career hinged on the public's need to drool over a half-naked hunk?

Yes. Yes, clearly her career did depend on a hunky fireman who couldn't even be bothered to tell her that he was being wooed by every modeling agency in Manhattan. Well, she wasn't going to let everything she'd worked so hard for go down in flames. Not without a fight.

She grabbed her cell phone from her bag and then hesitated with her thumb over the call button.

Do it, Carly.

She hit Call.

He answered. "Hey."

"Joe? What are you doing tomorrow?"

14

JOE HADN'T BEEN groped this much since he'd played tight end in college.

As Carly schmoozed from one end of the room to the other, he stayed by her side, nursed his beer and did his best to hide the fact that he would rather run into a blazing inferno than endure one more minute at this party.

He'd already spent the day being dragged from designers' studios to runway shows, listening to people talk about fashion as if it were the cure for world hunger. When he wasn't fending off modeling-agency reps who crammed their business cards in his pocket, he had to suffer being pawed at, fondled and propositioned by dozens of women and even a few men. He'd taken about as much as he could stand.

But Carly had asked him to come. And he'd wanted to see her. To watch her at work in her world. And she was incredible. Smart. Articulate. Knowledgeable. Even if the discussions about silk versus taffeta or cashmere, or the use of draping or bias cut or whatever made his eyes glaze over.

Carly glanced at him with a grateful smile and then nodded to the man she was talking with. She looked gorgeous tonight in a long strapless dress. The blue-green color reminded him of the water in the Caribbean. She'd pulled her long, brunette hair up in a twist that made him want to put his lips on that vulnerable spot on the back of her neck. Her stilettos and jewelry added a touch of sparkle, but it was her eyes he couldn't get enough of. They promised him a special reward once they got back to her place. And he was past ready to ditch this circus.

At her request he'd worn some designer suit she'd picked out for him. He took a swig of his beer. If one more woman scraped her long, fake nails down his cheek, or adjusted his tie, or asked him how tall he was, he might have to start drinking the strong stuff.

Carly winced, put a hand down on the table beside her and lifted one foot, rolling the ankle. Then she did the same with the other foot, dangling her shoe. Her feet had to be killing her.

He glanced at his watch. Three in the morning? They'd been at this since nine this morning. No, yesterday, now. Okay. Enough. Throwing one arm around Carly's shoulders and taking her elbow in his other hand, he smiled at the man who was telling Carly about the problems at his Milan studio. "Look at how late it is. Guess we better shove off, hon."

"But I—"

"Nice meeting you, sir." Joe nodded at the man, then

steered Carly to the right and guided her across the room toward the door.

"Joe, I was in the middle of a discussion." Carly tried to dig in her heels.

"I'm done here, Carly. And don't try to tell me you aren't beat."

She opened her mouth then closed it again. "All right. We'll go."

He stopped at the coat check, retrieved her wrap and his overcoat, and then stepped outside. "You hungry?" he asked as he raised his arm to hail a cab.

"No." She was clutching her thin wrap around her and shivering.

"You have to be." He shrugged out of his coat and draped it over her shoulders. "You've barely eaten a thing today." A cab pulled up and Joe opened the door.

"I was too nervous. Can you believe Michaela's assistant gave me an interview?"

"Why wouldn't he? You were the most beautiful woman in that room." He slid an arm around her waist to help her step over a pile of slush and get into the cab and then followed her in and gave the driver her address.

"So, it had nothing to do with the fact that I have a successful fashion blog?"

Backpedal, Tedesco. "Well, yeah. That goes without saying."

Her lips flattened as she threw him a disdainful look and he gave her his best sheepish grin.

And…it worked. She punched him on the shoulder but she was smiling as she shook her head. "Actually,

I wouldn't have gotten the interview at all if it weren't for you."

"No way."

"It's true. He wouldn't have given me the time of day if you hadn't been there. Everyone wants to meet the hunky new model that won my contest, and I made a deal with him to bring you in exchange for an exclusive."

Joe's brows shot up. He'd known why she asked him to go with her today. It's not as if she'd claimed to miss him. But he'd hoped that he meant more to her than arm candy and a means to an end.

"I should've told you about that when I called last night." Her voice had gone all quiet.

He shrugged. "I knew why I was here today."

"But you *were* planning on coming back to my place tonight, right?" Her hand slipped inside his coat and caressed his chest over his shirt. The one person he actually wanted running her hands all over him.

"Depends. You got anything to eat at your place? I'm starving."

"With all the food you ate at the party?"

"That wasn't food. Canapés are not technically food."

"Poor baby." She pouted.

Suddenly she leaned forward to redirect the cabbie. "All Night Bakery on Eighty-Second, please?" She glanced back at him. "You like bagels?"

"Throw in a couple of sausage sandwiches and you got yourself a sleepover."

She chuckled and snuggled against him, placing her

hand on his chest again. "You were really a good sport to come with me today."

"I wanted to be with you, Carly." Joe felt the tension drain from her body as he put his arm around her. He covered her cold hand with his and pressed his lips to her temple.

She reared back her head and looked up at him. "You know, you're a really nice guy."

He winced. "Hey, there's no call for insults."

She snickered as they pulled up to the bakery.

"You're still freezing. Why don't you wait here while I run in? What do you want?"

"Nothing for me."

"What about something for in the morning?"

She lifted one shoulder. "I'll take a bagel."

Joe hopped out and ended up adding a cinnamon roll to the order, as well as a couple of bagels for Carly.

Once they arrived at her building, he tried to pay the cabbie, but she insisted and he just didn't want to argue about it. She slipped her heels off halfway up the three flights of stairs, and by the time she pulled her key from her little sparkly bag she looked dead on her feet.

Joe followed her in.

"You want a drink? I have some brandy." She headed for the kitchen.

"Nah, do you have any—" He froze and cringed.

"What?"

"I was going to say milk." He held up the bag from the bakery. "With my sandwich."

She frowned. "So?"

"So, there goes my tough guy image."

She rolled her eyes. "Yeah, because firefighters are *so* not tough." She shook her head, and then turned toward her bedroom. "I may have some juice in the fridge. I'm going to shower."

By the time she came out of the bathroom in a silky black teddy, Joe was already naked and under the covers. She threw them off, stretched out on top of him, and began kissing down his jaw. "I see you're all ready for bed."

He grinned and patted her butt. "Don't even need a bedtime story."

As she nuzzled into his chest a yawn escaped her and she rested her head. "Sorry. Must be the champagne."

"Hey, we don't have to—"

"No, no. I just need to get my second wind." She kissed down his torso, but he cupped her face and lifted it to meet his gaze.

"That's crazy. You're exhausted."

She yawned again and stretched, sliding to his side. "I really am, but...you sure you don't mind if we just sleep?" Her index finger played with his nipple.

Sleep? Not if she kept doing that.

But he definitely liked being more to her than just stud service and a career boost. Something expanded in his chest. If he were prone to flowery prose he'd call it a warm glow. But basically he was just happy. He rubbed her back and kissed the top of her head. "Go to sleep, sweetheart."

Her only response was a soft sigh.

He smoothed her hair away from her eyes. She was

gone to dream world. He reached up to switch off the bedside lamp, and then wrapped both arms around her.

She felt so right nestled next to him. Her soft body lay alongside his, one long leg thrown over his thigh, one arm flung over his chest. Her breasts pressing against him. No way was he getting to sleep anytime soon.

Trying to distract himself, he stared around her bedroom. Light from her window showed the room in an eerie silhouette. Sirens blared and horns honked in the distance. They had maybe an hour before sunrise.

The room wasn't filled with expensive furniture, but it still looked as if it belonged to a minimalist. Warm and inviting was not her forte. In home decor or anything else, for that matter. But then, he already knew that.

He wasn't sure what it was about her that ignited such a fire in him. Hell, he wasn't sure he shouldn't douse the flames right now before he got burned. But he hadn't felt this way in a decade. And he'd like to believe she felt something, too.

She might claim that she'd only called him yesterday to help her career, but he'd heard the need in her voice. She thought she hid her emotions, but she wasn't always that good at pretending. She'd missed him.

His feelings for Lydia seemed like mere puppy love compared to the strength of his attraction to Carly. He and Lydia had been high school sweethearts. Known each other all their lives. Funny how, looking back, he remembered being so devastated when she broke it off with him. He'd spent years wallowing in bitterness.

And he'd kept himself closed off to another relationship ever since.

But even at his lowest, he'd always had his family to turn to for love and support. He couldn't imagine having to face life all alone. But Carly had. She'd managed to survive the wreckage of what her father had done and make a life for herself, without, it seemed, any help. And she'd thrived.

She knew what she wanted and went after it with single-minded determination. She was one tough woman. The kind of toughness it took to be a firefighter's wife.

Whoa. Wife?

But when she focused all that passion on him the rest of the world seemed to fall away. What if she put all that drive into a relationship? With him. Finding out seemed worth the risk.

Even if he ended up with third-degree burns.

MOIST LIPS WERE running over his body. A soft hand circling and tightening around his burning erection. But this was no erotic dream. Joe woke slowly, hard and aching with need. With a strangled groan, he pushed into the hand. Carly's hand.

"Morning, tough guy." Her voice was husky with sleep.

He managed a low growl as he slipped one spaghetti strap off and kissed her shoulder. "Morning." He rolled her beneath him and kissed her thoroughly, sliding his hand down her tall, slim body, taking the teddy with it. His fingers stroked her intimately, relentlessly, until she gripped his head and rocked her hips against his.

On his elbows, he held himself above her, cupping her face as he kissed her temple, her cheek, her jaw. And she kissed him back. There was something in her kiss this morning, passion, yes, always that, but he tasted need and longing. She seemed softer, more vulnerable. It gave him hope. Maybe she really could open up and let him be a part of her life.

Moaning, she urged him to her and he barely grabbed protection before he was inside her. He had to close his eyes it felt so good, so right.

Her throaty crooning of his name drove him over the edge and he thrust one last time, pulsing and trembling in ecstasy.

When he regained his senses he opened his eyes and gulped air into his lungs. "Carly?" His voice sounded dry and raspy.

"Mmm?"

"You okay?" He lifted his head from her shoulder. Her eyes were closed but she wore a half smile and her arms were still clasped tightly around his back.

"Mmm-hmm." She stretched against him and entwined her legs with his.

"I could get used to waking up like this."

Her eyes opened, and he read panic in them. So much for the softer, more open side of Carly. Her legs disentangled from around him and he obligingly rolled to his side while she scrambled off the bed and into the bathroom.

Damn. He got up and found his underwear. "Hey,

that's just an expression," he called, following her to the bathroom door. "I didn't mean that like, you know, I wanted to—"

She poked her head out of the bathroom. "What time is it?" she asked around a toothbrush. He heard the shower running. He checked the clock on her bedside table. "Eight forty-seven."

"Oh, I'm so late!" She disappeared inside the bathroom and he heard the shower curtain yanked back.

He let out a relieved breath. She was just late for Fashion Week. She hadn't misinterpreted what he said. But his mind had gone right there. He wasn't that serious about her yet. Yet? *Admit it, Joe.* He was thinking of her like that was a possibility. But it seemed way too soon. Obviously. But…someday? He shook his head and padded out to the kitchen. He'd had too little sleep to think about that now.

After making himself coffee and heating the other cinnamon roll, he poured Carly a mug and toasted her bagel, then brought them back to the bedroom. She was standing in the bathroom wearing nothing but a skimpy little black bra and panties. Her hair was already dry and she was putting on makeup. Man, what he wouldn't give to crawl back in bed for the rest of the morning.

"Aren't you going to shower?" She glanced in the mirror at his reflection.

Setting down her plate and mug, he shrugged. "I can after you leave."

She frowned. "Aren't you coming with me?"

"Today? Hadn't planned on it. I gotta be at the station early tomorrow for my shift and I have a pile of laundry waiting."

"Oh." Her face a mask of indifference, she pitched her makeup inside a flowered bag and sprinted for her closet.

He watched her go, but didn't follow. "Do you really need me there today?"

"No, you're right. I shouldn't have assumed." Her tone was flat as she pulled out two hangers, one with a skirt, the other a top, and held them both up, eyeing them together.

He scrubbed a hand through his hair. This hot and cold act of hers was driving him crazy. What were they doing here?

Gathering his clothes off the chair in the corner, he shoved his legs into the suit slacks and yanked them up.

She stilled, slowly lowering the two hangers. "What are you doing?"

"I'll shower at home." He slid on the dress shirt, buttoning with more speed than accuracy.

"What's the matter?"

She was so passive-aggressive he couldn't accuse her of anything specific. "I don't play games, Carly. I mean what I say and I say what I mean."

She spun to hang the outfits on a closet-door hook and then faced him, folding her arms under her breasts. "And I don't?"

"You want me to come with you today, but instead of saying so, you go all cold and indifferent."

Her lips tightened and she narrowed her eyes. "What am I supposed to do? Beg? I did that yesterday."

"You didn't have to beg. I enjoyed being there for you."

She scoffed. "It sure didn't hurt your career, either."

"What are you talking about?" He tucked his shirt in and zipped the slacks.

"You claim you don't play games, but you never mentioned to me that you'd had offers from modeling agencies."

"That's because I haven't." He sat in the chair and yanked on his socks.

"Right. Several modeling reps told me this week that they'd contacted you with offers."

"Well, they're ly—" Wait. He stopped tying his shoe. Several reps had tried talking to him yesterday, but he wasn't even there Thursday or Friday. "You mean, before yesterday? Contacted me how?"

Carly frowned and perched one knee on the rumpled bed. "Well, they usually call, but if they don't have your cell number they'd probably send a letter."

Joe thought back to all the letters that had come to the station. His sisters had left them on his coffee table, but after reading the first couple of creepy offers from strange women, he'd pitched the rest in the trash unopened.

"If they sent me letters, I didn't see them. I threw out a bunch of weird fan mail the day I got back from the cruise." He finished tying his shoes.

"Well, then, it's a good thing you were able to connect with them yesterday."

Straightening from the chair, he stood and shook his head. "Man, you're really bad at this, aren't you?"

She frowned. "At what?"

"At relationships. What part of me hating those photo shoots didn't you get? I don't want to model for anyone."

Her mouth dropped open. "You're right. I should've known that." Studying the bed, she grabbed a pillow against her chest and curled her arms around it. How could she look so vulnerable and so sexy at the same time?

"And if you were so upset that I kept a secret from you, why didn't you say something before now?"

Lifting her gaze to his, she shrugged. "That's just the way people are. They lie, they keep secrets."

Uh-huh. She must've learned that firsthand from her old man. He stalked to the bed and stopped in front of her. "I don't lie, Carly. And I don't keep secrets."

She stared at him, blinking. In her eyes he read disbelief. But he also saw hope.

He bent and raised his palms to her face. "Carly, I—"

Her buzzer rang.

Joe sighed and dropped his hands. She gave him an apologetic smile, slid off the bed and dashed out to her intercom.

He grabbed her robe off the chair and followed her, draping it over her shoulders as she pushed the talk button.

"Yes?"

"Carly, it's me. Buzz me in."

Carly stumbled away from the door, her mouth open and dread in her eyes.

He took her shoulders. "What's wrong?"

She blinked up at him. "It's my mother."

15

THE BUZZER RANG AGAIN.

What was her mother doing in New York? She hadn't mentioned a trip when they'd spoken last week. But Mother never visited unless something was wrong.

"Aren't you going to let her in?" Joe reached for the intercom.

"No!" Carly knocked his hand away. She couldn't deal with her mother right now. She was supposed to be at an up-and-coming designer's studio in fifteen minutes. Not to mention she was still reeling from the fight with Joe. Of course she was bad at relationships. That's why she didn't want to get involved with anyone. This whole thing with him was getting too complicated.

"Carly, it's freezing outside. You can't leave her standing out there."

He was right. She closed her eyes and summoned a last vestige of fortitude. Glaring at Joe, she huffed out a breath. "Fine." She pressed her palm on the buzzer.

Then she strode back to her bedroom to get dressed. She refused to face her mother in her underwear and robe.

When Joe followed her, she grabbed his suit jacket and tie still draped over the chair and offered them to him. "You need to get out of here."

Joe hung the tie around his neck and then slipped on the coat. "I want to meet her."

"Believe me. You don't." She ditched the robe, found a pair of black tights in her lingerie drawer and sat to pull them on.

"I thought she lived in New Mexico."

"She does. I don't know why she's here. But it can't be good."

"She's that bad?"

"You have no idea." She stood and pulled the check jacquard pencil skirt off the hanger and slipped it on, then reached for the black wool-and-cashmere sweater. "We don't get along. My family wasn't exactly all happy-happy, okay?"

"Well, maybe my presence will help."

Hah! "Joe, you don't understand. The woman will chew you up and spit you out." She sat to zip her boots. She did *not* want Joe to witness just how dysfunctional the relationship was.

Standing, she smoothed down her sweater and gave Joe a pleading look. "Please go?" A loud knock sounded at her door. She froze, her stomach fluttering. She gave Joe a withering look, set her shoulders and went to answer the door.

"How could you leave me standing out there in this weather? And in this neighborhood?"

"Hello to you, too, Mother." She stepped back, widening the door.

Her mother sauntered in, dropping an enormous bag on the bar. "Oh, you have company?" Her gaze slithered over Joe, who was leaning a shoulder against the door frame leading to the bedroom. "I know you. You won Carly's contest."

"Mother, this is Joe Tedesco. Joe, this is my mother, Victoria Herzberg."

"Call me Vicky." She smiled at Joe, and then shifted her gaze to Carly. "Not bad, Lee." She wiggled her brows.

Carly felt sick to her stomach. "You didn't let me know you were coming, Mother." The woman with whom she shared DNA had had more work done since Carly had last seen her.

"It was a last-minute trip." She smoothly removed her fox-fur coat and draped it over a bar stool. "I hope you're getting a new place soon." She eyed the tiny one-bedroom apartment as if it might transmit a communicable disease. "My friend Louise says she just listed a to-die-for apartment overlooking the park."

What alternate universe did her mother live in? "I can't afford something like that."

Vicky waved a hand, several brilliant rings catching the light. "But someday soon, darling."

Whatever *that* meant. Carly moved to grab her parka off the hook by the door and stuck her arms in. "Mother, I have to go. Why don't I meet you for lunch at your hotel?"

Her mother's surgically enhanced lips pinched in irritation. "But I just got here. And I had this wonderful idea while I was reading your little blog thing."

Her 'little blog thing'? "It's Fashion Week, Mother." Carly pulled her cell from her bag, checked the time. "And I'm late."

"Well, that's perfect. Your stepfather had some optometrists' seminar in Dallas, so I decided to take a trip, too, and do some shopping in New York. I want you to introduce me to all those designers you talk to." She beamed.

Carly clenched her teeth. "I can't do that, Mother. Tickets have to be purchased months in advance. Appointments arranged. It's not like dropping in on the neighbors."

"But I thought you could get me in since you're like the press or something. I want to see all the runway shows. It's so boring in Taos after the holidays. Gerald is busy with work, and all my friends are traveling."

Ah, her mother was bored? Well, at least her latest husband hadn't thrown her out. "I'm sorry, but there are no tickets left. You could come back in September."

Her mother's expression hardened. "I didn't think you could be so petty. You just can't let anything go, can you? You're still mad because I dared to remarry and move away."

"This has nothing to do with that, Mother."

"It's because I didn't take you with me. You know we just needed some time alone in the beginning. You could come visit now anytime you wanted, but you're always too busy."

Carly's face was flaming hot. She was shaking and

nauseated. All too familiar reactions to her mother. She pressed a hand to her stomach and tried to breathe deeply. "Mother, that's not why. I can't get tickets because they're sold out."

"Fine. I'll stay here with Joe." She cast him a sultry look. "You'll keep me company, won't you, handsome?"

Bile rose in Carly's throat. Joe unfolded his long body from the doorway and moved closer to her—and the door. "Actually, I've got to get going, too."

"Tell you what, Mother, I'll meet you for lunch at the Atrium at Lincoln Center. Some of the designers might eat there between shows, and I'll introduce you. Joe, don't forget your overcoat." She widened her eyes at him and he stepped around them toward the sofa.

"They *might* eat there?" Her mother's whine had taken a hard edge. "All I wanted was to see a runway show. Even if they are sold out, you're important enough to pull a few strings for your mother, aren't you?"

Carly bit her tongue to keep from cursing. Anything she said right now would only escalate the tension. She had to get out of here. "No, I'm not. And, I really have to go now." She reached for the doorknob.

Her mother held her wrist. "You always were a selfish brat," she sneered. "Your father spoiled you rotten, and you're just like him."

Carly wrenched her wrist away and threw open the door. "Get out."

Her mother didn't bother to try to hide her venom. "You think you're such hot stuff now that your blog is so famous?"

Joe stepped beside Carly and slipped his warm

hand in her cold one. "Mrs. Herzberg, I think you better leave." His tone was polite but clear as he stared pointedly at her.

Her mother glared at Joe, gathered up her coat and bag, and then marched out, chin raised high.

Wow, what a piece of work that woman was.

Joe shut the door, barely refraining from slamming it.

Carly just stood there, staring at nothing as she rubbed her wrist.

He wasn't sure what to say. He couldn't imagine growing up with a mother like that.

She might've once been beautiful. Tall and slim, like Carly, and striking, with her brunette hair and ice-blue eyes. But the artificial attempts to remain youthful-looking had ruined her best features, turning her face into a grotesque mask.

"Boy, that explains a lot, right there."

Carly scowled. "What's that supposed to mean? Now you know why I'm such a witch? Mystery solved!"

"No!" He slid his arm around her waist, but she wouldn't look at him. Her expression remained sad, but her body trembled. He ached for her. Wanted to make her pain go away.

"Hey." Joe turned her, wrapped her in his arms and held her tight, running a hand down her hair. "Carly, look at me."

She shook her head and avoided eye contact. "I need to go."

With a gentle touch under the chin, he lifted her

face. "You know I didn't mean it like that. You want to talk about it?"

"No, thanks." She huffed a laugh then hitched her purse higher on her shoulder, opened the door and stepped out. He followed, and as she locked it behind them, she turned to him and smiled, but it was such a patently false effort. "Actually, you're right, you know."

He frowned. "I told you—"

"No, it's the truth. I am really bad at relationships."

Oh, man. He gently squeezed her hand. "I shouldn't have been so harsh."

"Hey, you're not the first person to notice, believe me. You should run away from me as fast as you can." She pushed his hand away and looked him square in the eyes. "Because I'm just like my mother."

Geez, the expression on her face. He'd never seen her look so...so shattered.

Before he could deny it, she raced down the stairs. Joe went after her, called to her, but she didn't wait. He caught up to her at the curb but she'd already flagged down a cab and opened the door. She glanced back at him with a pleading look. "I'm so late. I need to go, okay?" Without waiting for him to answer she hopped in and it drove off.

He stood on the sidewalk trying to decide what to do. Had he been too hard on her, telling her she wasn't good at relationships? He wished now he'd never said anything.

All day he texted her, but she didn't reply. Without knowing her schedule he'd never find her. He thought about waiting at her apartment, but maybe she needed some time. But by the next day she still hadn't answered any of his texts. When he called, it rolled straight to voice mail. He left another message as he sat on the couch at the station with the other guys watching some show on TV. He must've sounded like a real sap but the guys didn't razz him for calling her every hour. They just gave him worried looks and kept silent.

He couldn't concentrate on the TV show, and he was less than worthless playing foosball. He kept thinking about Carly and everything that had gone down yesterday.

Had he blown it? Expecting too much? He'd rushed things. When he thought about it, he realized they'd only known each other a few weeks. It seemed much longer.

All he knew for sure was that he wanted to see her again. That he couldn't stop thinking about her. How brave she was, and smart and creative, and determined in spite of her mother. Joe knew she'd always be successful no matter what she'd been through with her dad. He wished she was here right now. With him.

He clutched the phone in his hand, but he wasn't going to call again. If she wanted to talk to him, she'd text or—

The alarm clanged and Joe jumped up with the rest of the guys. He sprang into firefighter mode, throwing on his gear and hopping on the truck.

As it rolled out, some of the guys were calling their wives, letting them know they might be late getting home. Joe pulled up a picture of Carly on his phone.

For the first time since he'd become a firefighter, he had someone he wanted to call.

But she didn't want to hear from him.

16

CARLY CLOSED HER laptop and then curled up on the sofa, rubbing her feet. The blog was done for tomorrow. She stretched and yawned. Yesterday had been a long day. Followed by an even longer day today.

But the phone call from *Modiste* had given her a jolt of energy to last a week. Evidently Joe's popularity with the fashion world had overshadowed any concerns they had about being associated with the name Pendleton.

She owed him such a huge debt of gratitude.

Thankfully, she hadn't heard from her mother again. Maybe she'd finally managed to tick her off so badly she'd stay away. Which seemed like a horrible thought to have about one's mother. Joe was so right about her. She was selfish, just like her mother. Her throat tightened just thinking of Joe.

She grabbed the remote, clicked on the TV and flipped through the channels. Anything to take her mind off his messages, especially the voice mail.

She'd played it back four times today just to hear

his voice. Why *he* was apologizing to *her* she had no clue. He was the best guy she'd ever known. The best person, period.

Too nice for her to mess up his life, that was for sure.

He must've finally given up on her since she hadn't replied. The last text she'd received from him had been early this afternoon. He'd said they needed to talk and to please call. But this was for the best. She had no idea what to say, anyway.

Her eyes were stinging again. It was after two in the morning. She had another designer studio showcase in less than seven hours. She should go to bed.

As she started to click the power button on the remote, a news report caught her eye and she clicked the power back on. A video of a multistory building on fire played in the upper right corner while the newscaster talked. The words *Firefighter* and *Critical Condition* scrolled across the bottom.

The newscaster was reporting on a fire in an office building in—she quickly turned up the volume—Brooklyn. He was talking about several firefighters being treated for smoke inhalation, and how the office building had been empty except for a cleaning crew. "The blaze appears to have been caused by faulty wiring and required the joint efforts of several companies to contain the inferno."

Inferno? The television swam before her. What Ladder was Joe a part of? And why didn't she know that? She didn't even know where he lived in Brooklyn. Geez, she really was self-centered, wasn't she?

The weekend news anchor continued. "The fire,

which started around six this evening, was updated to seven alarms by ten o'clock, and raged through the entire five-story building in the South Slope neighborhood, leaving three New York firefighters seriously injured. All three were transported to Park Slope Medical Center and are still in intensive care.

"And in other news, Vice President…"

Seriously injured. Critical condition. Carly muted the TV and grabbed her phone. She scrolled to Joe's name and pressed Call. He was probably fine. There was no reason for her stomach to squeeze so.

It rang twice, and then rolled to voice mail. No. She texted him.

Just heard about fire in Brooklyn. R U OK?

The next couple of minutes passed in slow motion. She jumped off the sofa and paced, dividing her attention between flipping to a different news channel and watching for mention of the fire, and checking her phone.

Forget this. She wasn't waiting for a reply.

She darted to her bedroom. Where were her snow boots? And she needed a cab. What hospital had the newsman said? She panicked. No, she remembered. It was Park Slope. She grabbed her coat and purse and raced out the door, already a flight down before she realized she was wearing old, ratty sweatpants and a sweatshirt from college.

And she didn't care.

She hailed a cab and directed him to the Brooklyn

hospital. As the cab bounced over icy ruts in the road, she stared at her phone, waiting for a reply.

Nothing.

It was almost three, now. His shift started at five yesterday morning and he worked twenty-four hours, so he should still be on duty at the station. If he hadn't been called to the fire, why wouldn't he answer?

Still no reply.

If anything happened to him, she'd... Her heart thumped. Panic made her catch her breath. She didn't want to lose him. What if she'd missed her chance?

No one had ever treated her as if she mattered until Joe. And, an astonishing realization, no one had ever mattered as much to her as Joe did. In just a few weeks he'd grinned and protected and cared his way into her heart.

Now, she was hyperventilating. The cabbie was looking at her as if she might fall apart before he could drop her off.

Take deep breaths, Carly.

She straightened in the seat. Tried to think about how the city skyline looked from this vantage point on the Brooklyn Bridge. She twisted to look out the back windshield. This is what Joe saw every day. He'd grown up in Brooklyn. Right across the river from her. But they might never have met...

The longer she went without a reply from him, the more convinced she became that something bad had happened.

By the time the cab pulled up to the hospital, she'd composed herself. She wasn't going to fall apart or make a scene. She paid the cabbie and walked in with as much dignity as someone wearing old sweats and clunky snow boots could muster and asked at the information desk for the names of the firemen who'd been brought in earlier.

"Are you a family member?" the elderly volunteer asked.

"Uh, no."

The volunteer gave her an apologetic look. "I'm afraid I can't disclose that information to anyone but family."

"Then, can you direct me to the ICU waiting room?"

The lady gave her directions and Carly thanked her and managed to not break into a run until she was out of the lady's sight.

She raced down the corridors until she saw the sign and darted to the left, down another endless hallway that ended abruptly at a set of double doors with a sign that read ICU Waiting. Carly pushed through them and headed for the nurses' station, hoping somebody would tell her something. But no one occupied the desk. Frustrated, she whirled to scan the room, hoping to find a firefighter's family member who might give her information.

An older couple. A woman with her arm around a child. An elderly man. Her search stopped on a firefighter's yellow pants with suspenders over a white undershirt. Joe. He was bent over in a chair, his elbows on his knees and his head in his hands. He was sooty and disheveled.

And so very much not hurt.

She cried out, and clamped both hands over her mouth.

And then she fell apart.

JOE HEARD A feminine cry and looked up. What the… "Carly?"

Her hair was pulled back in a messy ponytail and her cheeks were wet from tears. Her shoulders shook. He stood and rushed to wrap her in his arms. "Hey, don't cry now, it's okay." He kissed the top of her head as she buried her nose in his chest and sobbed.

"I thought you were hurt." She choked out between sobs. "I saw it on the news."

He had to smile. "And you were worried about me?"

"You didn't answer! I called and I texted."

He pulled his cell from his pocket and checked. It was still turned off from when he'd gone in to see Wakowski in ICU. "I forgot to turn it back on, I'm sorry." His shirt was getting wet from her tears. And he loved it.

"Stop apologizing." She cried harder and tightened her hold around his waist.

She cared about him.

She dug into her purse, fished out some tissues, and reached up to wipe his face, blackening the material with soot. "You're not hurt?"

The worry in her eyes put a big lump in his throat. He shook his head. "Nah. I'm fine."

"Then what are you doing here?"

"It's my buddy, Wakowski. He fell through the floor. Got a lot of internal injuries."

"I'm so sorry. Is he going to be okay?"

"We don't know. We're waiting to find out."

He'd been sitting here in the waiting room alone. So worried. His thoughts going to dark places.

He'd tried to comfort Wakowski's wife, but her mother was with her and they'd been allowed to sit in his ICU room. Her sister had taken their kids, and the rest of the guys had gone home to their families; relying on him to let them know when he heard any news.

Carly used another tissue to dry her eyes, but she only smeared the black makeup worse. He'd never seen her in these baggy old sweats, looking so sloppy. And she'd never looked more beautiful.

She sniffed and wiped her nose. "Can I... Is it okay if I wait with you?"

Damn. He was a goner, his heart another casualty from tonight's fire. He nodded. "I'd appreciate the company."

Several hours and cups of coffee later, Carly's head rested on his shoulder. Joe held her, cherishing her body's weight against him.

Tightening his arms around her, he was bursting to tell her he loved her, but was it too soon? Was he rushing things? Maybe right now was just a vulnerable time for her. Between her mother's visit, and the fear that he'd been hurt, she wasn't her normal, confident self. And he shouldn't take advantage of that. He wanted her to be clear about her feelings.

Well, maybe the same could be said for him.

"Joe?" Wakowski's wife, Sheila, called from the ICU doorway. She looked worn-out.

Joe shot to his feet, hopeful, scared. Carly stood, too. Her hand slipped into his. He swallowed. "How is he?"

A smile trembled on Sheila's lips. "He woke up. The doctor just checked him. He's going to be all right."

He was hugging her before he realized he'd crossed the room, picked her up and swung her around, grinning. As he put her down, Sheila laughed and patted his arm, then turned and disappeared back into ICU.

Wiping his eyes on his shoulder, he glanced behind him at Carly and then she was in his arms and he lifted her against him. "Let me text the guys, then I'll take you home."

She shook her head. "Let's go to your place."

"Don't you have to get to a Fashion Week thing pretty soon?"

"I'm not going."

"But what about your blog?"

"Oh! I can tell you my good news now." She fidgeted with excitement.

"What?"

"*Modiste* called and changed their minds. They're bringing my blog in-house."

He picked her up and swung her around. "That's great! Congratulations."

"And it's all because of you."

"Carly, your blog is your accomplishment."

"Yes, but it was your fame that made them forget who my father was."

"Fame?" He gave a look of skepticism. "I'm going to let the guys know Wakowski's okay."

While she gathered their coats and her purse, he

texted the rest of the ladder about Wakowski, then they walked out into a brisk morning. The sun was trying to fight through the clouds, sending patchy rays of warmth. A cab pulled up, but Joe held back when she would've opened the back door. An idea was formulating.

"What is it?" She waited, poised to slide into the backseat.

"Thank you for staying with me tonight."

She smiled. "You can make me breakfast." She climbed into the cab and he followed, directing the cabbie to his apartment. When he sat back and put his arm around her, she snuggled up to him, her eyes closed.

How should he phrase this? The subject needed delicate handling. "Carly?"

"Hmm?"

"Come to my parents' for dinner next Sunday."

She bolted away from him, all signs of drowsiness vanished. "Are you crazy?"

Okay, so, not the response he'd hoped for. "What's the problem?"

"I'm sorry, but were you not present when my mother paid me a visit yester—Saturday, whenever that was?" Her sarcastic tone lost its punch as she fumbled on the last few words.

"Carly, you are not like your mother. And I want you to meet my family."

She shook her head. "Not a good idea."

He took her hand, turned it over to brush his thumb over the soft flesh of her palm. "I care about you. And

I want to see where this thing between us might go. Don't you?"

She stared at him so long he figured she wasn't going to answer. He couldn't tell if the indecision in her eyes was good or bad. Then she turned her hand to clasp his. "What should I bring?"

17

CARLY'S FISTS WERE clenched so tight that when she forced herself to loosen them she couldn't open her fingers all the way.

Joe pulled up at the curb of a tidy, two-story brick house with a small front yard. The street was tree-lined, with a neatly shoveled sidewalk, and up and down the block kids were playing in the snow. Add a horse-drawn sleigh and the scene could've popped right out of a picture postcard.

Why had she agreed to this?

This past week she hadn't been able to think about anything else. Even the rest of Fashion Week had taken a backseat to being with Joe and worrying about meeting his family.

Joe came around the hood to open her door and then frowned when she didn't get out. "You all right?"

Carly sat frozen. She couldn't make herself move. Or answer.

"Carly?"

"I don't know why I let you talk me into this." Her voice trembled. She couldn't breathe.

He looked taken aback. "Be…cause you like my mother's cooking?" He flashed a grin.

"I'm serious, Joe. They're not going to like me."

He glanced behind him at the house, then heaved a sigh and leaned in, resting his forearm on the truck door. "They're going to love you."

Carly avoided his gaze, fiddling with the strap of her bag. "What if they don't?" Her stomach churned.

"Listen, my family needs to get to know the woman I love. But if it's going to freak you out this mu—"

"What did you say?"

"I said if it's going to freak you out—"

"No. Before that."

He grinned and leaned in until their lips almost touched. "You mean the woman-I-love part?"

She smiled. "Yeah, that."

His mouth covered hers in a slow, meaningful kiss. Her body relaxed, coaxed into his…and then he was straightening and stepping away. "Come on. Quit stalling." He offered his hand.

STALLING? HE'D JUST told her he loved her! That deserved at least a moment or two of consideration. He should be glad she wasn't running down the sidewalk screaming in terror.

And why wasn't she?

Before she could think of an answer he cleared his throat, crooking the fingers of his outstretched hand.

She took it as she stepped out, carefully avoiding

the pile of slushy snow with her Manolos. With a deep breath, she smoothed down her pencil skirt. It was probably too formal. She should've worn something more casual. She reached up to pat her hair. Now she was rethinking her French roll, too. Maybe she should've left her hair down. But it was Sunday dinner. Didn't people dress up for Sunday dinner?

She had no clue. Her family had never done Sunday dinner. Or any family dinner for that matter. Unless one counted dinner parties.

"You look beautiful." Joe smiled and put his arm around her waist to escort her to the door.

She pasted on her smile as the door opened and a short, plump, black-haired woman holding a baby threw her arm around Joe.

"Joey! We missed you last week. Oh, we were so worried about that fire. Good thing you texted Ma you were okay." She kissed his cheek with a loud smack and then stepped back and regarded Carly. "You must be Carly." Her smile dimmed as her gaze traveled down to Carly's shoes and back up again.

Oh, no, she *had* overdressed. The woman was wearing jeans and a bulky sweater.

Joe edged inside, bringing Carly with him. "Carly, this is my sister, Rosalie." He gestured at her, and then turned to point to each person in a small living room. "Rosie's husband, Ralph, my other sister, Donna-Marie, and her husband, Gino. My brother Al, and his wife, Linda, and my brother, Bernardo, and his wife, Mary Beth." All eyes were on her.

One of the women, the taller one that looked like Joe,

stepped forward with her right hand extended. "And there'll be a test on all our names later." She smiled as she shook her hand.

"Yeah, I shoulda made all you guys wear name tags." Joe moved across the room to help an older man struggling to rise from a recliner. "Carly, this is my father, Alfonso Tedesco Sr. Pop, this is Carly."

"Mr. Tedesco." Carly nodded.

Joe beamed at her as the older man shuffled forward, took her hand and kissed the back of it with dry lips. "*Benvenuti*. Welcome." He was tall and broad just like Joe and his brown eyes twinkled as he smiled at her. Then he turned to Joe. "*Molto bella,* Joey."

"I know, Pop." Joe nodded, meeting her gaze. The intense look in his eyes made her insides smolder. *He'd said he loved her!*

The baby started crying, Joe's sister—Rosalie— grabbed an enormous yellow-ducky-print diaper bag, and the rest of Joe's siblings returned to talking among themselves. The noise level in such a small house was nerve-racking.

A door slammed somewhere at the back of the house and Carly heard the stomp of what sounded like dozens of booted feet and the screech of kids.

The commotion got closer and within seconds children of every size from toddler to preteen stampeded in from the hallway and swarmed around her.

A fight-or-flight instinct kicked in. She stumbled back, warding them off with her hands palm out and a strangled yelp escaped.

The children—actually, the whole house—fell silent.

Carly glanced around the room. Everyone was staring at her as if she'd smacked one of the kids.

"I-I need to wash up." She threw a pleading look at Joe.

"Let me show you." He took her hand in his. Addressing his family, he told them to get started with dinner and they'd be right back, then he led her down the hall to a tiny bathroom.

Carly gratefully locked herself inside and turned on the water. Great. She'd been in the house less than ten minutes and she'd already managed to alienate everyone. And Joe wondered why she hadn't wanted to come here?

Calm down, Carly. Apologize. Blame it on stress. Fishing her compact from her bag, she dabbed powder on her nose, refreshed her lipstick where her teeth had scraped it off and then joined Joe in the hallway.

"You all right?"

"I'm fine."

Joe sighed and led her into an ornate dining room with a long oak table and matching hutch. Everyone was already seated around the table, except the children.

"Where are the kids?" she whispered to Joe. "I hope I didn't—"

"Nah, they always eat in the kitchen. No room for all of us in here." He held out a chair for her at the far end and took the seat beside her.

The woman she'd seen at the airport, his mother Carly presumed, was setting a large casserole dish of lasagna down in front of her husband, and then approached Carly, wiping her hands on her apron.

"So, this is my Joey's girl? Carly? So nice to finally meet you."

Finally? She'd only been seeing Joe a few weeks. Carly extended her right hand. "Nice to meet you, Mrs. Tedesco."

"Oh, *phtt.* Come here, sweetheart." Waving away the offered hand, she bent and hugged Carly. "And you call me Elena, okay?" She kept hold of her shoulders and embraced her. "Oh, you're even more beautiful than your picture."

Joe had showed his mother a picture of her?

"Now, I hope you're hungry because I cooked enough food for a football team and then Rosie and Donna-Marie brought more." Joe's mother took her seat and then looked at Carly expectantly.

"Yes, it all looks delicious." The woman wasn't exaggerating about feeding a football team.

Elena beamed. "Joey said you liked my lasagna recipe, so that's what I made today."

It seemed *Joey* had told his mother a lot of things about her. She opened her mouth to thank Elena when everyone bowed their heads, made the sign of the cross and then folded their hands.

Carly bowed her head.

Mr. Tedesco recited a prayer and everyone said, "Amen." And then dish after dish of food was passed around.

"So, Joey, how's Richie doing?" Elena asked.

"He's getting better, Ma. He's home from the hospital, and the doc says he'll be back at the station by Easter."

Richie must be his coworker, Wakowski. Carly tried to follow several conversations taking place at once. The father, Mr. Tedesco, was discussing "the shop" with one of Joe's older brothers. And Joe's sisters and sisters-in-law were talking to each other about their kids. One of them was in trouble at school.

"Don't worry. You get used to the craziness." The man to her right leaned in to speak sotto voce. He was one of the brothers-in-law.

Carly smiled and nodded. "How long did it take you?" She took a bite of salad.

"Me? Let's see, Rosie and I have been married… coming up on thirteen years this July. I remember 'cause we'd just gotten married a couple of months before the towers fell, and that Christmas Elena cried when we told her we were pregnant and Joey told her he was quitting college."

"Joey—Joe quit college?"

"Joey didn't tell you?"

"No. What happened?"

"You haven't heard this story yet?" The taller sister, Donna-Marie, called across the table. "Joey, you didn't tell her?"

"Ma, why don't you tell Carly how you and Pop met at Grandpop's tailor shop? That's such a good story."

"Now, Joey, don't try to change the subject. Carly, did you know Joey had a full scholarship to Notre Dame?"

Carly stopped eating midbite. She was aware her jaw had dropped open and shut it. "No." She turned to Joe on her left. "You gave up a full scholarship to Notre Dame?" How could anyone do that? She'd had to scrape together every dime she could get her hands on just to get through each semester.

He shrugged.

"The moron had a full ride playing football," his brother, Al, interjected. "Even had a recruiter from one of the top teams looking him over."

Carly turned her shocked expression on Joe again. "You could've gone pro?"

Joe opened his mouth, shaking his head, but his mother cut in. "Now, Al. You know how 9/11 affected us all." She shifted her gaze to Carly. "I admit I didn't want him to quit when he first told me. But now." She grasped his hand next to hers on the table and smiled at him. "I'm so proud."

"So." Carly was trying to process this new information. It changed everything she thought she knew about Joe. "You gave up a full scholarship to Notre Dame to become a firefighter?"

Joe frowned at his forkful of lasagna. "All those men and women running into the towers, saving people's lives, sacrificing their own. Playing a game for a living seemed so trivial after watching that." He lifted his gaze to meet hers. "I wanted my life to make a difference."

Something brittle inside her cracked. She blinked back tears. She'd never heard anything so selfless in her life. And to think this man said he loved *her?* Why? Any hope of coming out of this affair unscathed just died. Whatever part of her that was capable of love surrendered.

This was so not good.

18

JOE SET HIS forkful of lasagna back on his plate. This wasn't good.

In the past decade as a firefighter Joe had saved a few lives. Sometimes it was a cat, like last month. Sometimes human. It was the best part of his job.

The worst was becoming a headline when some reporter snapped his picture as he carried someone from a burning building. Thankfully, that had only happened once, several years ago. And, although his name had been mentioned, he'd still had his helmet on, so his face had been hidden.

Still, that look on someone's face, the expression of awe at his so-called heroics always made him uncomfortable. He figured he was just doing the job he'd signed on for. He'd never wanted fame and fortune. Give him a quiet life and a meaningful career and he'd be happy.

But now Carly was gazing at him with that kind of wondrous admiration.

Carly worried, he could handle. Carly turned-on was a great look. Even annoyed wasn't a bad thing. She wasn't some meek and compliant clinging vine. That was part of her appeal. But this expression she held now, as if he was some hero who was too good for mere mortals, or maybe just too good for her? He hated it. He wanted her to love him for who he really was: just a guy who loved her and wanted a life with her.

But she didn't say she loved you.

Shaking his head, he picked up his fork again. "It's no big deal. So, how's the business doing, Pop?"

His father frowned. "Not so good, Joey. Mr. Weitzman's been working on our taxes. Al says it's the recession, but I'm worried. We've never had such a bad year."

"What kind of business do you have?" Carly directed the question to his pop at the other end of the table.

"Like my father before me, and his father before him, we are tailors. My grandfather, Giuseppe Tedesco, came to the United States from Lombardy, Italy. He taught his son, who taught me." He clapped a strong hand on Al's shoulder. "And so I teach Alfonso."

Joe had heard the story a million times, and today the pride shining in his pop's eyes was no different.

His brother, Al, nodded, his pride also evident. "And my oldest son, Roberto, is already proving to be very talented with a measuring tape."

Pop's face drooped. "But what if we have no shop to leave him? Every year we have fewer customers."

"Things will pick up, *amore mio*." Ma reassured him, but everyone at the table had fallen silent.

"Maybe you could run a special on your website to draw in new clients," Carly suggested.

Everyone's attention turned to her. Again.

"We don't have a website," Al said.

"You're kidding? Everyone needs a website nowadays. How do people find you?"

"Tedesco's Tailoring has been in our neighborhood for generations. Everyone knows where we are." Pop's chest puffed out.

She blinked, her face blushing light pink. "Of course. I'm sorry. It's none of my business."

"No, please. This is a great idea." Al's enthusiasm was clearly reflected in his voice. "Maybe a website could bring in more customers."

Carly's eyes lit up with excitement. "Well, I could set one up for you easy."

Al glanced at their father. "Pop?"

Pop narrowed his eyes. Folded his arms over his chest. *Say yes, Pop.* Joe willed him to agree.

The old man stuck out his chin and gave an imperial nod. "Yes, we do this."

Carly grinned and glanced at Joe as if to gain his approval. He lifted an arm across her shoulders and squeezed.

She scanned the table. "Does anyone have a laptop?"

Ralph scooted back his chair and stood. "Mine's out in the car." He headed out front and Carly started talking about domain names and web hosting.

Joe sat back to observe his family's growing excitement and then stared at Carly. His love for her deepened into a profound sense of rightness.

Shoot. He'd probably end up having to thank his sisters for entering him into that contest.

"OKAY, SO WE mentioned fully lined suit jackets, and on the shirts you offer French cuffs, monograms and what else?"

"Collars, we do over ten collar styles," Al answered, leaning over her shoulder as she typed on Ralph's laptop.

"Now, about wedding gowns?" Al Sr. pointed a finger at the screen. "We'll have a…a page for that?"

"Oh, yes. Let's add that to our menu." Carly began typing, but Elena bustled into the upstairs bedroom that had been converted into a study and placed a firm hand on her shoulder.

"Now, Alfonso, that's enough for tonight. Carly is tired, and Al, your wife is ready to take the children home."

Carly blinked up at her surroundings. It was dark outside and the house was quiet. What time was it? She checked the clock on the laptop. Eleven-thirty! "Oh, my gosh!" She jumped to her feet searching the tiny room. "Where's Joe?"

"He's fine. Watching basketball with Bernardo and Ralph downstairs."

Rosie and Donna-Marie poked their heads in the doorway. "Good night, Pop," Rosie said. "Carly, it was nice to meet you." Donna-Marie waved then turned to yell down the hall. "Kids, we're leaving, get your coats."

Joe's mother hugged Carly. "Thank you so much for all you're doing for our family." She kept an arm around

Carly's shoulder and guided her out of the bedroom, heading toward the stairs. "Now, I want to send some cake home with you. You're too skinny." She winked.

A medium-size kid came barreling out of another bedroom, almost crashing into his grandmother. "Georgie!"

"Sorry, Grandma!" He raced down the stairs.

Donna-Marie was stooping to pick up a smaller child who had fallen asleep in front of the TV. Another kid was still playing with a video game controller, his avatar leaping over a ledge.

Carly took in all the football trophies lining the top of a tall, scarred chest of drawers, and filling every flat surface from a bedside table to a small desk. Without thinking, she stepped inside.

"Roberto, turn it off now." Donna-Marie held the one child against her shoulder while she used her free hand to drag the last child from the room. She turned back at the door. "Good night, Ma, good night, Carly."

Joe's mother hugged and kissed her daughter and grandkids, then stepped inside the small bedroom. "This was Joey's room until he went off to college. After Bernardo married, Joey had it all to himself."

There were posters of bands and a sexy blonde in a bikini hung on the walls. Carly soaked in all the information about Joe's childhood preserved like a mini-time capsule.

Wooden bunk beds with matching navy blue plaid comforters. A baseball glove hanging over one of the bedposts. A mini-basketball hoop hooked over the closet door.

She spied a framed photo hidden among the trophies on the dresser of a young girl in a high school cheer-leading outfit posing in the arms of a young Joe wearing a football uniform. His high school sweetheart? She picked it up, studying the blonde beauty with the turned-up nose and the self-assured smile.

"That's Lydia." Joe's mother was staring at the photo, as well. "Joe was going to marry her."

A wave of jealousy hit Carly square in the chest. Was that a wistful note she detected in the mother's voice? The girl in the picture looked to be everything Carly wasn't. Warm. Friendly. Loving. "What happened?"

"She dumped me." Carly twisted at Joe's deep voice. He was leaning in the doorway holding a plate with cake slices covered in clear plastic wrap. His expression was somewhere between amused and accusatory. So he'd caught her trying to pry information from his mother. Could he blame her?

"I'll say good night, now." Joe's mother leaned in and wrapped her arms around Carly. After a few awkward seconds Carly finally relaxed and put one tentative arm around the older woman's back.

Elena let go, stepped away and smiled. "It was so nice to meet you, Carly. Please come back again." She hugged Joe next. "Good night, son."

After Elena had left, Carly realized she still held the framed photo and set it back on the dresser. "The game is over?"

"Yep. Pop went to bed. Said to tell you good night and thank you again." He set the plate on the desk and then gazed at her with that heat in his eyes again.

"It was fun, actually. I was happy to do it."

"You can't understand how much this might mean to my father. Other than his family, the shop is everything to him. To lose it after three generations would break him."

She shook her head. "I can't imagine knowing my family's history back that far. I don't even know my grandparents."

"None of them?" Joe sounded incredulous.

Was that so unusual? She shrugged. "My mother's mother was a single mom. Mother never knew her dad and my grandmother died before I was born. My father's parents quit speaking to him after he married my mother. And once I was born, and they wanted to see me, my father wouldn't let them. Said they didn't deserve to know me."

"Whoa. Talk about holding a grudge."

"Yeah, in case you hadn't already guessed, I come from a long line of dysfunctional characters. You should run away. Far away." She tried to sound flippant, but the warning was dead serious.

"Too late." He slipped his arms around her and kissed her, moving his mouth over hers in a sensual play of give-and-take. "I'm already hooked." He held her to him, pulling her head to his chest.

Warmth spread inside her, reaching into dark, cold places she hadn't even known existed. Was there any better place to be than in his arms? *I love him.* She was still getting used to the feeling. Definitely not something she was ready to say out loud. *But he'd said it to her.*

But what about what's-her-name? She glanced at the photo of the happy couple. He must've loved her, too, if they'd planned on marrying. Maybe he was one of those guys that fell in love at the drop of a hat. Maybe the cheerleader had just dumped him recently and Carly was the rebound lover. The coldness returned like fog rolling in off the Hudson River.

"Tell me about her."

"Who? Lydia?"

"No, the woman on the poster. Of course, Lydia."

He chuckled. "Are you jealous?"

She pushed away from him. "Don't get cocky. I'm just curious."

His skeptical grin told her he didn't believe her. But he drew her over to sit on the bed with him. Clasping her hand in both of his, he held it in his lap and sighed. "It was a long time ago." He scanned the room as if remembering the past. "I'd come back to live at home, and been training at the Fire Academy for a few months. Lydia was attending Kingsborough and both of us were working. We'd hardly seen each other since Christmas when I'd told her about quitting Notre Dame.

"She'd been acting kind of distant and I thought she was mad that I hadn't given her an engagement ring for Christmas. So, I thought I'd surprise her for Valentine's Day." He winced.

"I bought a ring and drove to her parents' house, but she wasn't home. They said she was studying, so I waited."

A muscle ticked in his jaw as he studied their joined hands. "Finally about midnight she gets home." Clicking his tongue in disgust, he looked away and ran a hand through his hair. "I got down on one knee and everything." He sighed. "She turned me down, saying I'd changed the plan midstream. She didn't want to stay in Brooklyn her whole life. She'd planned on being a pro-ballplayer's wife."

Carly shook her head. "What an idiot."

He threw her an incredulous look and barked a laugh. "Me? Or her?"

"Her! For letting you go."

A slow smile curved his mouth as he leaned over her and then urged her down to the mattress, his lips almost touching hers. "Does that mean you won't let me go?"

She trailed a finger over his dark brow, down his stubbled cheek and then combed her fingers through his hair. "Maybe."

With a growl he took her mouth. Powerful and possessive, exploring her with his tongue. He moved his lips down her jaw to her throat, kissing along her neck to take her earlobe between his teeth.

She reached under his jacket and tugged his shirt out from his slacks, running her hands over his ripped abs up the solid muscles of his chest. Without lifting his mouth from her neck he began unbuttoning her blouse. When she started helping he moved his hand to reach under her skirt and caress her thigh. He groaned. "Carly? Are those stockings and garters?"

She smiled. "Yes."

He groaned again, rolled off and got to his feet. "Let's go back to my place."

Rebuttoning her blouse, she sat up and raised a brow, teasing him. "You don't want to do it in your old bed?"

"I never disrespected my parents when I lived here and I'm not going to start now."

"So, you never…? With Lydia?"

"Of course not." He acted disgusted and Carly's heart sank. What? Lydia had been too pure for sex? Whereas Carly had slept with Joe merely because he got the wrong room number.

He grabbed the plastic-wrapped plate from the desk and headed for the door. Then he turned back with a lopsided grin. "We did it in the backseat of my car like any self-respecting teenagers."

Happiness launched her off the bed and into his arms. She jumped up, wrapping her arms around his neck and her legs around his waist. "Take me home, Firefighter Joe."

His eyes crinkled as he smiled. "Yes, ma'am."

Oh, how she loved this man. It scared her to death how much. And how quickly he could demolish her.

And that was the problem, wasn't it? He made her deliriously happy. But inevitably, she would fail him.

And the thought of hurting this wonderful guy? How would she live with herself?

19

"WHAT THE...?" Joe mumbled to himself as he stared at his cell phone. Twelve texts! And it was only 7:00 a.m.

He'd just stepped out of the shower when the phone went nuts. The first text was from his brother, Bernard, who worked in the city. Joe felt the life drain out of him. It was a picture of himself on the jumbotron in Times Square. He was bare from the waist up, wearing only tight black pants and tall pirate's boots. Ten stories tall!

Across the top were the words *Brooklyn's Sexiest Fireman.* Great. He'd never hear the end of this from the guys.

Carly had taken that picture of him in the Caribbean. The photo shoot had been sponsored by *Modiste,* but the words scrolling across the bottom of the jumbotron *was Carly's blogsite web address.* How could she have sanctioned this?

HE COULDN'T READ one text before he had three more. And that was in between answering calls. His sisters, his other brother, his sisters' friends. Rosie told him she saw the photo everywhere she looked on the internet. The stupid photo had gone viral.

He nearly smashed his cell against the wall of his apartment.

He tossed it on the bathroom counter just as he noticed his chief's number. This should be fun. The chief told him there were women and reporters outside the fire station, their cars obstructing the drive that by ordinance had to stay clear for the fire trucks. The team had gone out to get them to move their cars, and reporters had asked the guys for interviews.

Geez, it was barely nine in the morning.

"And guess who I just got off the phone with, Tedesco." Chief didn't wait for Joe to guess. "The fire commissioner. Keep your mug away from the firehouse until this crap dies down. And while you're at it you might want to decide whether you want to be a model or a fireman."

Joe clenched his teeth, his fists ready to pound something. "Yes, sir," Joe said, but the line was already dead.

He needed to see Carly. Half of him wanted sanctuary. The other half wanted an explanation.

This morning she'd left for her place just after dawn, even though he'd tried to persuade her to stay. But it was her first day working for *Modiste*. He'd understood. But when he'd tried to make plans to meet her for lunch later, she'd hedged and said she'd call him. Had she known *Modiste* was going to put his photo up in Times Square? Was that why she'd raced out of his apartment?

He threw on some old jeans and a sweatshirt, and

hurried down the stairs. But once outside he heard shouts. "There he is!" He snapped his gaze up as a group of women, flanked by a bunch of reporters rushed toward him, converging on him like a crazy mob ready to lynch the village monster.

Some reporter shoved a microphone in his face and a woman tried to grab his coat. There were less than a dozen people there, but for a moment he imagined the small crowd swarming over him like ants on a carcass and him getting devoured alive.

Man up, Joe.

He braced himself for the onslaught, ignored the reporter shouting questions and ducked his head as he braved the gauntlet to get to his truck.

Before he could make it, another female almost tore his coat off. Camera phones flashed, and a video camera was recording as he fought his way inside his truck.

He locked the door and ran his hands through his hair. He was shaking as he looked down at his torn coat. What was wrong with people?

He headed for the Brooklyn-Queens Expressway and drove straight to Carly's apartment. He had to circle her building twice to find a parking spot. At least there weren't any mobs outside her place. He hit her buzzer, then stomped the slushy snow off his boots.

"Yes?" Her still sleepy voice came over the intercom.

"It's Joe."

The door unlatched and he took the stairs three at a time, striding down the hall until he reached her door. She was waiting for him in her open doorway with a huge smile. Before he could say anything she threw her arms around his neck and planted a deep kiss on his mouth. "What are you doing here? Did they call you, too?"

"Who? What's going on, Carly?"

Her smile vanished. "You sound mad. What's the matter?"

He took her hand, tugged her inside her apartment and closed the door. "You tell me." He wanted to hear this from her lips.

"Joe, what's wrong? *Modiste* just called me. I was going to text you."

"Oh, yeah? So, you didn't know they were going to do this until this morning?"

Her brows crinkled and she cocked her head. "How could I? But, I thought you'd be happy for me."

"Happy? I was just mobbed outside my apartment. The chief is threatening my job." He pointed at his coat. "They almost took this off me!"

Carly blinked. "Mobbed? What?"

"You really didn't know about the jumbotron? You didn't choose this picture?" He snatched his phone from his pocket, brought up the picture and held it in front of her nose.

Frowning, she took the phone from him. And gasped. "I didn't. Oh, my God." She gasped again. "They told me my blog's URL was scrolling across the bottom and I was just excited about getting that kind of exposure." She grinned. "You have to admit you look pretty good."

Joe grabbed the phone back from her. "There were crazy women blocking the fire station this morning.

Chief told me to stay away and decide whether I wanted to be a model or fireman."

Her mouth dropped open. She turned, walked to the club chair and sank into it. "I'm sorry. I didn't know."

He closed the distance between them. "Carly. You have to get that picture off the jumbotron."

She looked up at him. "Me? I have no control over what *Modiste* does."

"Talk to them. Give it a shot."

Her expression hardened. Her eyes had never looked so icy as she gazed at him. "You thought I somehow did this, and then didn't tell you?"

"It crossed my mind, yeah."

Carly refused to let Joe see how much she ached right now. Why wouldn't he assume that? Her father was a liar, right? And they'd already established that she was so selfish she couldn't make a relationship work. But it still hurt. Like a phantom pain in a missing limb, she wanted to rub her chest where a normal heart should be.

She nodded. "Fair enough. Like father, like daughter?"

His jaw muscle ticked and he stepped back, placing his hands on his hips as he lowered his gaze. "That's not what I—" He growled under his breath. "Carly."

Tired of him towering over her, she stood and paced to the kitchen for a moment. What she was about to do required a clear head.

Joe followed.

She refused to let her jumbled emotions get the better of her. "I tried to warn you, you know. No. Actually, you told me." Putting a finger to her temple, she cocked her head and squinted. "If I recall correctly, you're the one who said I was bad at relationships. So, it's not like you should be surprised."

"Come on, Carly. That was before."

"No, you come on, Joe. We both knew this was never going to work between us."

His expression darkened. "No, I don't know that."

"Eventually I would've really screwed things up, right?" She took a long breath and released it.

"No." Joe stalked around the bar, tried to take her in his arms, but she flattened a palm on his chest to keep him away.

"The truth is, even if I could make *Modiste* take down that billboard of you in Times Square, I wouldn't."

He flinched, just briefly, but she caught it. His eyes narrowed. "I don't believe you."

"Why would I? It's going to make my career. My chance to make it big. You really think I'd choose you over that?" She held his gaze, calling on every ounce of anger she could muster, willing him to believe her lie.

He smiled, shaking his head. "You're just trying to prove a point. Okay, I get it. I shouldn't have assumed the worst about you." He spun and ran a hand through his hair. "And you're right. I was upset. It's been a weird, crazy morning. I've never faced a mob like that."

Carly gestured at the door. "I think you should leave."

He spun back around. "The hell I will."

She had to harden her nonexistent heart. If he didn't get out of here soon, she might not have the strength to make him. Her throat ached trying to swallow past a huge lump. It was all she could do not to press herself against his strong chest and beg him to forgive her and kiss her and hold her and stay with her forever.

Wow. Two months ago she would have told this new, sentimental Carly to snap out of it and get a life. And that's what she needed to do now. Since when did she let a man dictate her career?

And her former self was right. Her life would be so much easier to manage without all the mess and fuss of having to deal with another person's baggage.

Yeah. Right.

He was staring at her. "We'll talk about this later once we've both calmed down." He dug into his coat pocket and pulled out his truck keys.

"It won't change anything." She schooled her expression and gave him a weak smile.

His lips flattened as he stepped close to her again and kissed her. His mouth lingered until she succumbed and softened hers, committing the feel and scent of him to memory.

She didn't move until he stepped away and took a few hesitant steps backward. Until he'd spun and strode out the door and the sound of his boots clomping down the stairs had faded; then she unfroze and squeezed her eyes closed.

Goodbye, Joe.

20

"I'LL SEE YOUR dollar and raise you three." Wakowski shoved four white chips into the middle of the card table.

Joe eyed Wakowski. Was he bluffing? His buddy held his gaze and grinned.

Joe studied his hand.

"You guys need more beer?" Wakowski's wife called down from the top of the basement stairs.

"Nah, babe, we're about done for the night," Wakowski called up to her. "As soon as I wipe the floor with this rookie." He chuckled, then grabbed his side. "Ow."

"You're supposed to take it easy after major surgery, dimwit," Stockton said.

"Hey, I been doing nothing *but* taking it easy. I know it's time to go back to work when I can sing the theme songs to all my kids' favorite cartoons."

Joe smiled. The poker game tonight had been a great idea. Take his mind off everything that had happened.

Since he'd left Carly a few days ago he'd called her twice, but it just rolled to voice mail. All his texts went unanswered. Déjà vu all over again.

One reporter and a few fanatics still hung out at his apartment and the station. The chief had said Joe could work his next shift since the commotion had died down. But he'd been adamant about making sure there were no further incidents. If only Joe hadn't made such a big deal about the whole thing to Carly.

"So, what youse gonna do, Tedesco?" Miller had folded and was supposed to have been home thirty minutes ago. His wife kept texting him.

Everman leaned back in his folding chair, puffing on a cigar. "Yeah, you gonna bet sometime before Christmas, Mr. Sexy?"

Stockton smacked Everman on the back of the head.

"Ow!" Everman scowled and rubbed the spot where he'd been hit. "What?"

His fellow firefighters avoided Joe's gaze, glancing at each other uneasily.

"It's okay, guys. It happened. I'm over it." What a load of malarkey. What he wouldn't give to have Carly texting him to hurry home. In fact, he'd settle for any kind of text. But just like her father, that woman sure knew how to hold a grudge.

In his family, you got mad, you yelled at each other awhile and then you worked it out. You didn't break up at the first sign of trouble.

He pushed all his chips into the center of the table. "I'll see your three dollars, Wakowski, and raise you everything I got."

Stockton whistled. "High stakes there, Tedesco."

Wakowski shook his head. "Oh, no, I ain't falling for that again. I thought you were bluffing last time. I fold." He threw his cards on the table.

Joe grinned, and showed his hand. His Jack-high straight was missing the nine.

"Oh, for the love of—" Wakowski cursed, and all the guys got to their feet, complaining.

Joe raked in his chips.

"Hey, watch out, Tedesco." Everman called out as he headed for the stairs. "You know what they say. Lucky in cards. Unlucky in lo— Ow!"

Stockton walloped Everman on the side of the head as they both climbed the stairs.

Joe paused as he scooped the chips off the table into a plastic bag.

"Don't pay him any attention, Joe." Wakowski waved a hand at Everman's retreating form. "Everyone knows he's a doofus."

"Hey, I told you. I'm over it." Joe shrugged, pretending the old superstition hadn't made his chest tighten. "Carly was just a…" He couldn't bring himself to say the lie out loud. A fling. An affair. A good time while it lasted.

"Yeah, sure." Wakowski nodded his understanding of the sentence left unfinished and stood gingerly, holding his side. "No big deal, right?"

"Right." Joe agreed. Just because he'd felt a kind of magic when he was in her arms. And he'd imagined little rug rats with his black hair and her ice-blue eyes. And told her he loved her.

He came around the table to assist his buddy. "Want a hand up the stairs."

"I'm fine." Wakowski shooed him away.

"Richie, let Joe help you, or you can sleep on the couch tonight…" His wife called down the stairs.

Wakowski sighed, rolled his eyes and made a face at Joe as if to say, *You see what I have to put up with?* "Yes, dear." He yelled back.

Joe grinned, even as his chest ached. He wanted that. The good-natured nagging, the kids' toys scattered everywhere, the woman who loved him so much she let him go downstairs to play poker when he was supposed to be resting.

But maybe it just wasn't meant to be for him. The woman he wanted didn't want him.

He shook off the self-pity. *Move on, Joe. You'll meet somebody else.*

Maybe.

Someday.

He patted Wakowski on the back as he took the guy's weight on his shoulder. "You're one lucky guy, Wakowski, you know that?"

CARLY UNCLENCHED HER fists and made herself step out of the cab, walk up to the Tedescos' front door and knock. She'd come straight from a meeting at *Modiste's* offices today, so she was, once again, overdressed. Her stomach twisted. Good thing she hadn't eaten anything since the small spinach salad at lunch.

It would be okay. Al Jr. had promised her Joe wouldn't be there tonight. She couldn't face him. She dreaded even having to face his family. He'd probably told them everything. They seemed like the kind of family where secrets were a rare commodity. But, she'd promised to come back and finish their website.

The door flew open and Joe's mother greeted her with a warm smile. "Carly, so good to see you again, thank you for all your help." She enveloped her in long hug, embracing her affectionately. As she started to let go, Carly clung to her, squeezing her eyes closed. She'd never had another woman she could confide in. No mother to comfort her. And she suddenly, powerfully felt what she'd been missing all her life.

"Aw, sweetheart." Elena held her tight, rubbing her back until Carly got control and stepped away. Maybe the woman wouldn't notice her sniffle.

"I made calzones." She took Carly's coat and then ushered her into the kitchen. "I thought we'd eat before you guys get started."

The kitchen smelled of garlic and oregano and sizzling butter. Her stomach was growling from the enticing aroma. Carly hadn't thought she could eat, but now…

Als Sr. and Jr. both joined them in the kitchen as Elena pulled a baking sheet from the oven, instructing Carly to have a seat at the table. She set the dish on a hot plate in the center of the round laminate table and then poured Carly and Al Sr. a glass of tea. A bowl of salad and a basket of garlic toast joined the main dish and Elena took a seat. Carly's mouth watered.

Al Sr. said the prayer, and then everyone lifted their heads.

"So, how's your new job going?" Elena asked. "Is it everything you hoped?" Elena stared at her expectantly, giving her a friendly, interested smile. Hadn't Joe told her about their breakup?

"Um, I love it. *Modiste* has brought in a 3-D techie who's revamping my blog to include virtual shopping, and I met with him today."

Elena nodded. "Ooh, 3-D? That must be exciting."

"It is." Carly searched Elena's features for a hint of anger or disapproval, but the woman acted as if everything was fine. What was going on?

Joe had stopped texting a couple of days ago. So, he must've accepted that they were over. But she longed to ask her how he was. Was he still missing work? How was he handling their breakup? Was he upset? Or relieved? But she just took a bite of the delicious meal and sipped her tea.

"Since the website for our business has been up, we've already had more customers." Elena covered Carly's hand with hers and squeezed. "I hope you know how grateful we are. You're so wonderful to do this." Her eyes misted over and she blinked and returned her attention to slicing bread.

Carly had no idea what to say to that. Wonderful? Her?

The conversation turned to the website and the pages Al Jr. still wanted to add, and soon they were upstairs talking about custom bridal gowns and alterations for every article of clothing under the sun. Once again, Elena came upstairs to check on them when it got late. But Carly felt good about the site now. She recommended someone who would maintain and update the website for a nominal annual fee, and both Als shook her hand, gushing about her kindness and generosity. She felt like a fraud.

"You'll come to dinner this Sunday with Joe?" Elena took her arm in hers as they traveled down the stairs.

Carly froze. What? Okay, she had to be honest with this dear woman. "Uh, Elena, you know Joe and I are no longer seeing each other, right?"

"Oh, *phft*. Joey said you had a misunderstanding." She waved her hand in dismissal. "Couples fight. Then they make up. That's love. You and Joey just need to talk."

Love? People who really loved each other trusted each other, didn't they? They didn't assume the worst, and blame the other person for things beyond their control.

Or choose their careers over their loved one.

Did they? How could a relationship recover from that?

"I don't think talking would help, Elena." Carly stopped at the bottom of the stairs. She had an irrational urge to weep on this woman's shoulder and pour out her heart. If only talking to Joe would help. Now that the idea for hope had been presented, she realized she'd shut down her emotions so she wouldn't have to feel the devastating pain. "I said some awful things." Her voice broke.

Elena transfixed her with a steely-eyed stare. "Tell me, do you love Joey?"

Carly blinked. Did she? She thought about the agony

of the past week. She'd been walking around in a gray fog. Miserable. Cold. Just existing.

Then memories flashed. Of Joe in the Caribbean, making love in the pool of the cave, of him coming to her rescue when she had the panic attack at the cruise terminal. Of him bringing her dinner when she was miserable over her dad's scandal.

Whenever she was with Joe the icy wall she usually kept around her heart melted away and she was able to let love and warmth and color into her life. She liked who she was when she was with him. She needed him in her life.

She loved him.

"Oh, Elena, I do." She stared in awe at Joe's mother. "What do I do? I want to make this work."

"Aw, *caro.*" Elena threw her arms around her. She patted her back and let Carly cling to her. "Where there's true love there is always forgiveness."

"You think he'll forgive me?"

"Of course, *figlia.* He loves you. Go to him."

Digging a tissue from her bag, Carly dabbed at her eyes and nodded. "Okay." Her mind was racing. What would she say? Would Joe let her in? Was he even home? Maybe Elena could help.

JOE STANK.

But the fire was finally out. It'd blazed for over fifteen hours and he hadn't been home in over thirty-eight. He was exhausted and filthy. But it felt great to be back doing what he loved. The public had finally turned its attention to the next big thing. At least until the May issue of *Modiste* came out.

Finishing off the burger and fries he'd picked up on his route home, he parked his truck and trudged up to his apartment. It was only early evening, but all he wanted was a shower and bed.

As he entered his dark apartment he thought he detected the faint scent of Carly's fragrance and his throat constricted. Cruel thing, the sense of smell. Just one whiff could bring back so many memories. She'd only been here once, the night before their disastrous fight. Maybe his mind was playing tricks on him. Just wishful thinking.

Gritting his teeth against the heartache, he headed straight for the bathroom, shed his clothes and spent long wonderful minutes with the hot water pulsing over him. Teeth brushed, he remembered to text his ma to let her know he was safe. He thought about adding a question about Carly's visit. But he let it go.

Ma had called a couple of days ago to let him know Carly was coming over there that night to finish the website for Pop. She'd specifically mentioned that Carly had asked if he would be there, and that the "poor thing" seemed as if she just needed some time.

Translation: Don't come over.

Joe growled as he unwrapped the towel from around his waist and padded naked down the hall to the bedroom. What did Carly need time for? It wasn't as if she'd lost her temper and needed to cool down. The woman had been as cold as ice when she told him to leave. He wished she would lose her temper. Then they could yell at each other, get it all argued out and then spend the rest of the night making up.

But there was no melting the layer of frost Carly had built around her heart.

The apartment was dark, but he didn't need light to find the bed. He dropped onto the edge of the mattress with a weary sigh. He stretched aching muscles and lay back, sticking his legs under the sheet and folding his hands behind his head. Maybe he could try to call her one more time tomorrow. Or maybe he'd just show up at her apart—

"Long day?"

Joe jumped and nearly fell off the side of the bed. The mattress dipped and a silhouette moved toward him.

He peered into the dark. "Carly?" He reached behind him and turned on the bedside lamp. And blinked. "What—"

She scooted closer and laid a hand on his chest. "Don't throw me out yet. Please, listen?" She wore a black silky bra and panties that hugged her curves and exposed the creamy flesh of her cleavage.

He swallowed and forced his gaze back to her face. "Okay."

She bit her lip and studied her nails. "I've been on my own so long. The only example I had of how a relationship worked was my parents." She pulled a face. "Not exactly sterling role models. But that's a child's excuse. You showed me it could be different. I know it won't be easy, but I'm smart." She gave a half smile. "I promise I can learn. I don't want to live without you in my life."

Joe couldn't believe she'd come to him, was actually saying words he longed to hear.

"Joe?" She looked scared. "Say something, please?"

"Uh, Carly?"

"Yeah?"

"You had me at 'long day'." He rolled her under him and took her mouth, moving his lips over hers, savoring her like a starving man revels in his first bite of food.

Carly moaned and hummed her desire, returning his kisses with a fiery passion. Had he thought she owned a frost-covered heart? He'd been so wrong. She was hot and loving in his arms and he moved between her legs while he trailed his open mouth down her throat. "Carly, I'm sorry I lost my temper."

"Shh, I'm the one who should apologize. You had every right to be upset. I should've been thinking of you instead of myself." She placed frantic kisses along his temple, his jaw and finally on his lips again.

He pulled away and gazed intently into her eyes. "Promise we'll talk things out from now on. Don't go all cold on me again."

Bringing her palms up to frame his face, she nodded. "I promise. Just please forgive me."

"We have to work things through. Just don't clam up."

"I'll try to remember that we can always work things out if we love each other."

Joe stilled. "What was that?"

She grinned. "Oh, did I forget to mention that part?" Her smile faded and her expression turned serious. "I love you, Joseph Michael Tedesco." She pulled his face down for a sensual lingering kiss.

He took her wrists and pinned them to the bed on either side of her head. "Say it again."

"I love you."

With a low growl he folded his arms around her and held her tight against him. "Carly. I love you so much."

Joy was a living thing thumping in his chest. He didn't think he'd ever been so happy. Groaning into her neck, he slid a hand up from her waist to cup her perfect soft breast and push it into his waiting mouth.

She cried out as his tongue circled her tight nipple over the bra. "Off," he murmured. "Take this off." He tried to lift it over her head, but she had to help, as his hands shook. She tossed it and her panties onto the floor while he grabbed a packet from his bedside drawer.

"Oh, Joe." She reached down to guide him inside her and he was home. Surrounded by her warmth, cushioned by her body, completely at one with her in this moment. "My sexiest Average Joe."

He stilled. "That's not funny."

She giggled. He'd never heard her giggle before. "It's a little funny."

"No." He teased her earlobe. "Not even a little." He pressed into her.

A throaty little cry escaped her. "You're right." She held on to his firm butt with both hands, bringing him back to her. "There's nothing average about you, Joe."

He smiled down into her eyes, thrust deep and she gasped.

"Yes." She moaned and moved her hips in rhythm

with his. Once he'd started moving he couldn't, didn't want to stop. Carly hooked her legs around his waist and he suckled a breast until she was calling his name, and stiffening with her orgasm as he climaxed hard.

Sinking into the mattress, Joe let the pleasure wash over him. He nuzzled Carly's cheek, catching his breath.

She moaned, caressing the back of his neck until he shivered.

"I want to go to bed with you every night and wake up with you every day."

Her fingers curled into his hair. "And I want to eat at your parents' house every Sunday and watch every game with you." She kissed his eyes, his nose, his mouth.

He frowned. "How'd you get in here, anyway?"

"Your mother gave me her key. Did I mention that I love her, too?"

"No, but that's probably a good thing."

She sighed and snuggled close as he rubbed her back. "I'm so glad you crawled into the wrong bed."

He grinned. "Best mistake of my life."

Epilogue

PIPER DID A double take as she walked past the magazine stand on Madison Avenue. Her picture was on the cover of the May issue of *Modiste,* along with that fireman she'd posed with in the Caribbean.

Her stomach twisted as she recalled how badly she'd behaved on that cruise. On impulse she spun and retraced her steps. If she remembered correctly, the *Modiste* offices were somewhere around here.

Yes, there was a sign on the building. She rode up the elevator and asked for the editor. Half an hour later, she had what she wanted: The name and address of the poor woman she'd dragged into her scandal.

She worked from her home in Brooklyn, and Piper remembered now, she had a fashion blog. Piper hailed a cab and used the ride out there to think about what she wanted to say once she saw Carly.

Asking the cabbie to wait, she found the apartment number and knocked on the door. Now that she was standing here, she thought maybe she should've just called. But, no. This needed to be done in person.

The door opened and it was the same woman, but she looked different. Her features seemed softer, her clothes more casual, and…a slow smile spread across her face. A warm, inviting smile.

"Uh…Ms. Pendleton?"

"Carly. Hi, uh…Piper. What's wrong?"

"Oh, nothing." Piper stood there, regretting her impulsive decision now that she was here. This woman probably didn't want to hear anything from her.

"Would you like to come in?" She gestured her inside and Piper straightened her spine and strode in.

"Can I get you something to drink? Coffee? Soda?"

Piper smoothed her hair behind her ears. "No, thank you."

Carly sat, crossed her legs and indicated that Piper should take the other club chair in front of the fireplace. "What can I do for you, Piper?"

Piper glanced around. The place had a homey feel to it that she envied, and also didn't quite match with the woman she'd met on the cruise. She would've thought the woman would live in a high-rise in Manhattan.

She noted a laptop on a small desk in the corner, the scented candles burning on the mantle and a large framed photo of Carly wrapped arm in arm with— the fireman! They were both smiling into the camera, their faces so happy, it was obvious they were deeply in love. She met Carly's curious gaze. "You and the contest winner?"

Carly's face softened even more. Piper would go so far as to say she looked dreamy-eyed. "Yes. Sometimes I still can't believe such a great guy loves me."

Amazement mixed with envy as Piper soaked in the information. What must it be like to believe so completely in the goodness of someone? She couldn't imagine.

"So, what can I—"

The front door swung open and the subject of their discussion breezed into the apartment, a humongous greyhound on a leash beside him. "Max should be all tuckered out now," the handsome fireman called, then stopped abruptly at seeing her. "Hi."

The dog trotted over to Piper and stuck his nose in her lap.

"Max. Sit!" Carly ordered. The dog sat, his tail wagging and his tongue hanging out of the side of his mouth. It was the ugliest dog Piper had ever seen.

The fireman unhooked the leash and went to stand beside Carly, who'd gotten to her feet. He slipped an arm around her waist and touched his lips to her temple.

"Piper, you remember Joe?"

"Hey, Piper. What's going on?" Joe flashed an easy smile and extended his right hand.

Piper stood to take it briefly. "I should go."

"Oh." Carly scratched the animal behind the ears and the dog seemed to smile. "How's your little pooch?"

Pootsie? Piper hadn't thought of that dog in months. How silly that seemed now, to think a dog would fill the hole in her life. "I found a good home for her."

Carly nodded but Piper could tell the woman was confused. "Did you…need something?"

Need? What she needed no one could give her. Piper cleared her throat. "I only wanted to apologize for my behavior on the cruise. I'm sorry that I caused you pain. I've been…selfish."

She thought she heard Carly mumble, "Join the club."

"Hey, none of that, now." Joe's free hand rose to gently cradle Carly's cheek. Carly covered his hand with her own and gazed into his eyes with such…love.

"Apology accepted. It all worked out, believe me."

Piper's chest squeezed. "Yes, I can see that."

She moved to the door and Carly followed, opening it, and then laid a hand on her arm. "You know, we actually have you to thank for bringing us together. Good luck, Piper. I hope you find what you're looking for."

That wasn't possible. But Piper didn't say that. "Thank you. Goodbye."

As she climbed into the backseat of the waiting cab and directed the cabbie back to Manhattan, she remembered the serenity of the beach in Miami. The weeks she'd spent there with Ragi right after the cruise. Perhaps she should return there to seek what she needed.

Even if the peace was only temporary.

* * * * *

*Don't miss Piper's exciting sexy romance
available soon from Harlequin Blaze!*

REQUEST YOUR FREE BOOKS!
2 FREE NOVELS PLUS 2 FREE GIFTS!

HARLEQUIN *Blaze*®

red-hot reads!

YES! Please send me 2 FREE Harlequin® Blaze™ novels and my 2 FREE gifts (gifts are worth about $10). After receiving them, if I don't wish to receive any more books, I can return the shipping statement marked "cancel." If I don't cancel, I will receive 4 brand-new novels every month and be billed just $4.74 per book in the U.S. or $4.96 per book in Canada. That's a savings of at least 14% off the cover price. It's quite a bargain. Shipping and handling is just 50¢ per book in the U.S. and 75¢ per book in Canada.* I understand that accepting the 2 free books and gifts places me under no obligation to buy anything. I can always return a shipment and cancel at any time. Even if I never buy another book, the two free books and gifts are mine to keep forever.

150/350 HDN F4WC

Name _____ (PLEASE PRINT) _____

Address _____ Apt. # _____

City _____ State/Prov. _____ Zip/Postal Code _____

Signature (if under 18, a parent or guardian must sign) _____

Mail to the **Harlequin® Reader Service:**
IN U.S.A.: P.O. Box 1867, Buffalo, NY 14240-1867
IN CANADA: P.O. Box 609, Fort Erie, Ontario L2A 5X3

Want to try two free books from another line?
Call 1-800-873-8635 or visit www.ReaderService.com.

* Terms and prices subject to change without notice. Prices do not include applicable taxes. Sales tax applicable in N.Y. Canadian residents will be charged applicable taxes. Offer not valid in Quebec. This offer is limited to one order per household. Not valid for current subscribers to Harlequin Blaze books. All orders subject to credit approval. Credit or debit balances in a customer's account(s) may be offset by any other outstanding balance owed by or to the customer. Please allow 4 to 6 weeks for delivery. Offer available while quantities last.

Your Privacy—The Harlequin® Reader Service is committed to protecting your privacy. Our Privacy Policy is available online at www.ReaderService.com or upon request from the Harlequin Reader Service.

We make a portion of our mailing list available to reputable third parties that offer products we believe may interest you. If you prefer that we not exchange your name with third parties, or if you wish to clarify or modify your communication preferences, please visit us at www.ReaderService.com/consumerchoice or write to us at Harlequin Reader Service Preference Service, P.O. Box 9062, Buffalo, NY 14269. Include your complete name and address.

HB13R2

Read on for an excerpt from

Wicked Nights

by New York Times *bestselling author Anne Marsh.*

Piper was naked.

Okay, so she wasn't totally naked, but a man could dream.

Somehow, he'd timed his arrival at her slip for the precise moment she grabbed the zipper running up the back of her wet suit. Undeterred by his presence—because surely she'd heard him snap her name—she pulled, the neoprene suit parting slow and steady beneath her touch.

Hello.

Each new inch of sun-kissed skin she revealed made certain parts of him spring to life.

Even as he reminded himself that she'd spent most of their early days trying to either torment or kill him, however, his eyes were busy. Piper's arms were spectacular, strong and toned from hour after hour of pulling herself through the water and then back up into the boat. Now she was looking sexier than any stripper, uncovering skin that was a rich golden brown from time outdoors. The way she'd braided her water-slicked hair in a severe plait only drew his attention to the deceptively vulnerable curve of her neck.

But this was *Piper.*

So dragging his tongue over her skin and tasting all the

places where she was still damp from her dive should have been the *last* thing on his mind. He'd read her the riot act about her careless driving and say his piece about tomorrow's business meeting. Then he'd go his way and she'd go hers.

The wet suit hit her waist.

Neither short nor tall, Piper had medium-brown hair, brown eyes and a slim build. Those cut-and-dried facts didn't begin to do the woman in front of him justice, however. They certainly didn't begin to explain why he unexpectedly found her so appealing or why he wanted to wrap an arm around her and take her down to the deck for a kiss. Or seven. He didn't like Piper. He never had. She'd also made it plenty clear that he irritated her on a regular basis.

So why was he staring at her like a drowning man?

And...score another point for Piper. Like many divers, she hadn't bothered with a bikini top beneath the three-millimeter suit. His kiss quote rocketed up to double digits.

"Piper." His voice sounded hoarse to his own ears. *Focus.*

She jumped, her head swinging around toward him. "If it isn't my favorite SEAL."

**Pick up WICKED NIGHTS
by *New York Times* bestselling author
Anne Marsh.**

**Available October 2014 wherever
you buy books and ebooks.**

The EX Factor!

Kristine Zimmerman is finally divorcing the man she left years ago. Sean Maddock is even hotter now, but there's nothing left between them, right? Then he proposes a deliciously sinful weekend for old times' sake...and she can't think of a single reason to refuse!

From the reader-favorite

From Every Angle trilogy,

Close Up

by *Erin McCarthy*

Available October 2014 wherever you buy Harlequin Blaze books.

And don't miss

Double Exposure,

the first in the

From Every Angle trilogy, already available!

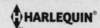

⊕ HARLEQUIN®

Blaze®

Red-Hot Reads

www.Harlequin.com

HB79821